✧ WITCH'S FANG

WITCH'S FANG

HEATHER KELLERHALS-STEWART

POLESTAR
BOOK PUBLISHERS

Witch's Fang
Copyright © 1994 by Heather Kellerhals-Stewart

Published by:
Polestar Press Ltd.
1011 Commercial Drive, Second Floor
Vancouver, BC
Canada   V5L 3X1

Excerpt from "David" from *Collected Poems* by Earle
Birney. Used by permission of the Canadian Publishers,
McClelland & Stewart, Toronto.

The Publisher would like to gratefully acknowledge the
financial assistance of The Canada Council, British
Columbia Cultural Services Branch, and the Ministry of
Canadian Heritage.

Editing by Jennifer Glossop
Cover design and illustration by Jim Brennan
Map by Jim Brennan
Production by Michelle Benjamin
Printed in Canada by Best-Gagne

Canadian Cataloguing in Publication Data

Kellerhals-Stewart, Heather
     Witch's fang

ISBN 0-919591-88-4
I. Title.
PS8571.E5862W5 1994   jC813'.54   C94-910127-3
PZ7.K46Wi   1994

To Markus Kellerhals

Thanks to Rolf, Erika, Markus and Fern
for reading the text and making suggestions.

We climbed ...
    ... because we had joy in our lengthening coltish
Muscles, and mountains for David were made to see over,
Stairs from the valleys and steps to the sun's retreats.

— Earle Birney
"David"

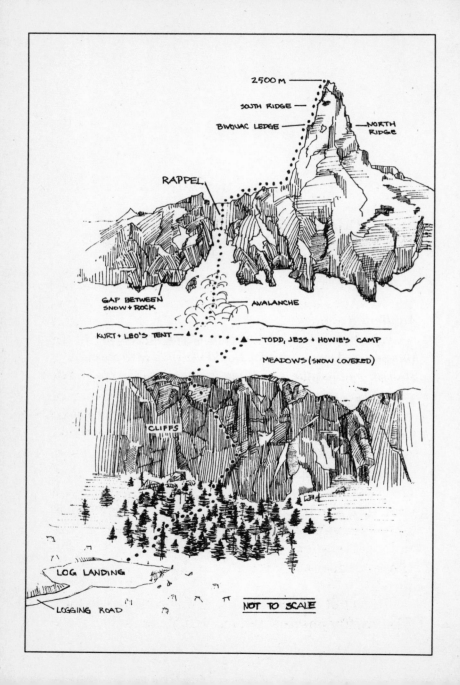

2500 M

SOUTH RIDGE

BIVOUAC LEDGE

NORTH RIDGE

RAPPEL

GAP BETWEEN
SNOW + ROCK

AVALANCHE

KURT + LEO'S TENT

TODD, JESS + HOWIE'S CAMP

MEADOWS (SNOW COVERED)

CLIFFS

LOG LANDING

LOGGING ROAD

NOT TO SCALE

✧ PROLOGUE

THE MOUNTAINS WERE BORN from a ring of fire into
the Ice Age — heat clashing with cold. Sometimes
the fire prevailed, sometimes the ice. Lava melted
vents through the ice sheet and flowed out to
congeal into rock. The sky, a witness to this violent
birth, was pelted with lava and plumes of fiery ash
until the clouds themselves burned red. Occasionally the young volcanoes rested, but always with
one eye open. Through the eons the ice came and
went, patiently gouging away at the fire-born rock,
and when the ice sheet retreated for the last time,
cliffs of basalt remained where heat and cold had
met. Too steep to resist the pull of gravity, these
massive walls sometimes crashed down on the
valleys far below. And with the weight of ice gone,
the volcanoes too grew still — fire and ice hand in
hand.

Rain fell, the sun shone, snow came and went.
The swiftly passing seasons left their mark on the

mountains. Moss campion, alpine anemone, saxifrage ... struggled for a footing in the bleak rock crevices and lower down on the slopes fireweed sprang up, with Douglas fir swift to follow. When people came at last, they kept to the river valleys as the wild beasts before them had done. The high places, where the wind howled around ancient lava flows, were left alone. But one day a mountain of rock and water cascaded down upon the valley bottom. Eyes turned upward in fear, and during long nights around the campfire, legends were born. What terrible spirits guarded those contorted peaks?

Then other people came and they did venture into the high places. Surveyors measured, recorded and marked the volcanic peaks on maps. A crazy breed of men and women, known as mountaineers, donned hob-nailed boots and climbed the Black Tusk, Mt. Garibaldi, Tricouni Peak ...

But one spire of rock, rising from the snow fields like an extinguished flame, stood untouched. They called it the Witch's Fang. Volcano born, weathered by ice, wind and meltwater, it had become a black, decaying tooth. Climbing parties sniffed around the cliffs, tested the serrated, knife-edged ridges and, in typical mountaineering understatement, decided it wouldn't "go." A few even hinted that it was unclimbable. For a while the Witch's Fang was left alone.

But the winds blew, the years moved along and the times were so ever swiftly changing. A new generation came along, young climbers who scaled sheer cliffs and ice falls, actively seeking out the most difficult routes. Some even climbed alone, without ropes or other aid. Before his car accident, Todd Rushton had been one of these climbers.

✧ CHAPTER 1

TODD'S FINGERS CLAWED FOR THE DOOR that swayed beyond him. His body felt numb, his mouth too dry for words. It was eerily quiet, except for a steady drip, drip, drip. His arms went limp and fell back on the mangled car seat. There was no pain — yet.

Pain! The word took shape inside a woman's spiralling scream and soaked into his body like the gas. It stank. The gas was everywhere, dripping across the dashboard, down his leg, into his running shoe. Or was it blood? If only that woman would stop screaming. Todd arched his body towards the door again. Something held him back.

"Let go, damn you!" Todd shouted.

He sensed a hand on his shoulder and his father's voice saying, "Take it easy, Todd. You must have been reliving the accident."

Todd opened his eyes. His head was resting

across a pile of books. Everything was exactly as he had placed it: the neat pile of chemistry-lab notes, eraser, pencils, two felt-tipped pens for writing on any surface, calculator. How could he have dropped off in the middle of studying for tests? That's what had caused the car accident in the first place — falling asleep at the wheel.

A couple of days off from tree planting, hot weather, a long drive to visit friends — tired, sure, but hardly reason to keel over at ten-thirty in the morning. How could he have fallen asleep at the wheel? Naturally the police suspected booze.

"Were you drinking?" an officer asked accusingly, hovering over his hospital bed.

"No, I wasn't. Can't you think of anything except drinking and driving?"

"Simmer down, Todd," his father cautioned. "You can't blame them for suspecting alcohol."

Great support he got from his family!

"I'll need to make a full report," the officer went on. "Can you outline the circumstances leading to the accident?"

His mind was still groggy from the operation, making concentration difficult. "Well, I guess I left the treeplanting camp around four-thirty in the afternoon. Drove till dark and set up my tent somewhere off the highway. Next morning I woke early, maybe five-thirty, and started driving. I wanted to reach my friend's place in good time."

"Todd, are you all right?" his father's voice broke in again.

"Sure, I'm fine." End of conversation. But it wasn't easy shaking off the shreds of the nightmare. Almost a year after the accident and he was still having them.

"Don't be so hard on yourself, Todd. I'm pushing fifty and I still relive the climbing accident that killed my best friend. Close my eyes and I'm back thirty years, watching his slow spiral through space and feeling my own mortality for the first time. Remember you're barely —"

"Seventeen," Todd interrupted, "with a foot that looks and feels like a hunk of meat and a permanent limp."

Sam Rushton sighed. "We've been over this how many times, Todd? You're lucky to be alive. The police and everyone have said it. You could be a paraplegic. You could have lost a leg, a foot. You escaped from a nasty accident relatively unscathed."

"Lucky? Oh, that's rich. I fall asleep in the middle of the day and total a car. But not to worry. There's nothing wrong with me."

"Well, if you want to wallow in self-pity, I can't help you. Better pull yourself together, Todd."

"I don't want to wallow in self-pity, as you put it. But you don't take me seriously, Dad. Nobody in this family does. Look, I have a bad car accident, almost kill myself, and I haven't been climbing since. If I didn't realize it before, I know now ...

climbing was my whole world."

"So what's keeping you from climbing?" Sam asked more gently.

Todd stared down at his foot. "Maybe it depends what you mean by climbing."

"How so?"

"You can't imagine what it's like being on a sheer cliff face all by yourself, putting up a new route. Way back, you just bushwhacked up the easiest ridge and called it a first ascent."

"It's the high places that matter," his father insisted, "not how you go."

"If that's what you think, why not go by helicopter, by plane?"

"That's not what I meant, Todd."

"Yeah, I know."

"You've been doing some hiking and skiing since the accident. Who's to say you won't rock climb again?"

"The doctors. Be realistic, Dad. I've got limited flexibility in my ankle."

"Things heal quickly when you're young. Besides, you've already proved the doctors wrong."

"Oh, sure, if all I want to do is climb some harmless little rock bump with a hundred other people."

"All I can say is, if you truly love something you don't give up that easily. You go back again and again until you've looked at it from every angle."

"Yeah? Well, you're sounding more and more like some school psychologist. I guess it never occurred to you that I might be scared — damn scared."

"Of course you are. It will feel as if you're starting all over, like that first day in the mountains — how many years ago now?"

Todd looked his father in the eye. "Do you think I can rock climb again?"

"Yes, but maybe not on your terms. Start with an easy climb. Go with someone you trust, someone who understands you and the pull of the mountains."

"Howie," Todd murmured.

"Yes, someone like your friend Howie. He's a careful, responsible climber. Why not go with him?"

"You keep talking about going. I'm not going anywhere."

"Talking of climbing," his father went on, "I've been meaning to show you this letter I got from the Seattle Mountaineers." He tossed an envelope onto the dining room table. "They want to climb the Witch's Fang and several other peaks in the area."

"You mean *the* Witch's Fang?" Todd asked unnecessarily.

Hey, wait a minute, the Fang was their mountain. Ages ago, before he could even walk, his father had carried him to the base of the mountain. Together, they had spent hours poring over old pictures, maps and air photos, and in their imaginations they must have climbed the Fang a hundred times. If it hadn't been for his accident, he might have tried the Witch's Fang this spring.

Todd grabbed the letter. "May ... they want to come in late May. But that's only two months away."

Formed by volcanoes, molded by ice. Fire and ice together ...

The words kept flickering through Todd's mind as he reread the letter. Fire and ice — the two ancient forces that cradled the world — fire and ice burning in his own heart.

His father was watching him intently. "The Mountaineers are wondering if there's any local interest in climbing the Fang. What do you think?"

"Don't look at me." Why did his father have to go and show him that letter?

"Sorry, I wasn't suggesting you should tackle the Fang. I just thought you might pass the letter on to some of the younger members in our Alpine Club. I'm sure Kurt would jump at the chance."

"You can't mean Kurt Stone, Dad! He's bad news on a mountain. Besides, he must be twenty-two at least — hardly young."

"I wouldn't wish Kurt on any climbing party either, but when he hears about the attempt on the Witch's Fang, wild avalanches won't hold him back." Sam sighed. "If I were a few years younger, I'd go myself. But my knees can't take the punishment any more. Pity — the Witch's Fang is the last unclimbed mountain within easy reach of Vancouver, and not many people realize this."

Todd's twin sister, Jess, swept through the kitchen door. "Did I hear someone mention the name of our most notorious rock jock?"

"I thought you were supposed to be practising ballet, Jess."

"I was doing my exercises upstairs. But when people are arguing, it fills the place with bad vibes and upsets my balance."

"Dad and I were talking, Jess."

"Some gathering we have here," Norma Rushton remarked, dodging Jess as she spun through the kitchen. "I don't see any cooking action. Whose turn is it?"

"Hers." Todd pointed to Jess.

"We were discussing Kurt Stone," Jess explained.

"We? Dad and I were peacefully talking until you butted in, Jess."

"That will be the day when this family discusses anything peacefully," Norma observed, "politics, the environment, climbing — you name it."

"We agree on Kurt," Jess reminded her. "He thinks women are a nuisance on trips, plus women go climbing only to snag a man."

"Stone Age man," Norma agreed.

Sam stifled a laugh.

"It's not funny, Dad. What colossal egos you guys have! No wonder women are going on their own trips into the mountains."

"Don't go blaming Kurt on Todd and me," her father pleaded. "We aren't responsible for his behaviour."

"Nobody likes climbing with Kurt," Todd said,

coming to his father's rescue. "But going back to the Witch's Fang — do you think the Mountaineers stand a chance of climbing it?"

"Difficult to say, Todd. Spring is definitely the time to go. The bush lower down will still be under snow, and with any luck the snow on the steep slopes should be well consolidated. Plus the fact you young rock-jocks are tackling routes I wouldn't have looked at."

"Scratch me from the rock jock category," Todd muttered.

"What a climber on the Fang needs is luck, plenty of luck," Sam rambled on. "Luck with the weather, luck with falling rock, luck with route finding. Plain skill isn't enough. Trust no hold on the Witch's Fang. Still, I'd say the Mountaineers have some chance of climbing it."

Todd tried to blot out his father's words, but they kept returning to attack like a swarm of blackflies. Why couldn't he wipe the image of that rotten mountain from his mind? Fire and ice ... Oh, cut the melodramatics. He was in no shape to climb the Fang now. Weeks of hobbling around on crutches might have swelled his arm and shoulder muscles, but they had also withered his leg muscles and wrecked his sense of balance. Hiking — that's what he was good for now.

"Would Howie be interested?" Sam's voice intruded into his thoughts again. "I have complete air-photo coverage for the area around the Witch's Fang."

"I don't care if Howie is interested. Let's drop the topic, okay?"

Long silence. Jess's ballet music filling in the background — Tchaikovsky as usual.

"Dinner," she finally announced.

Welcome diversion, even if it was her tuna-and-noodle casserole.

"For a ballet dancer, you show uncouth signs of hunger," Todd teased her.

"To carry on a conversation with you, brother dear, I need energy."

After supper, Todd barricaded himself behind a pile of books on the kitchen table. He glared at Jess between furtive chews on his pencil. She had nabbed the tape deck again and was playing "Swan Lake" full blast. Would no one stop her?

"How's the swimming going, Todd?" Norma asked.

Oh no, not another interrogation session ... "I didn't go this afternoon, Mother."

"Didn't the physiotherapist say you should go every week?"

"There wasn't time after my doctor's appointment. Besides, I had a headache."

"That's too bad. You could try drinking some coffee when you feel an attack coming on."

"It wasn't a migraine, Mother."

"What did the doctor say?" Sam barged in where Norma had left off.

"He said there still isn't enough flexibility in my ankle, that I may need another operation eventually and ... oh, I might as well give up working around here." Todd slammed his chemistry book shut and escaped upstairs.

"A mite touchy this evening," Sam remarked.

More indistinguishable conversation from downstairs. "Swan Lake" came to an end. At least Tchaikovsky had the decency to shut up.

Upstairs, Todd burrowed into the map cupboard and pulled out the air photos that covered the area of the Witch's Fang. He fitted the two adjoining air photos together until they were slightly overlapping, then positioned the stereo glasses above the connection. Todd focused on the Witch's Fang. Bang! As if speared on the tip of a horn, he was tossed skyward and just as abruptly dropped into the chasm below. Todd shook his head. The peak looked so fearsome that he had to keep reminding himself how stereo magnifies the steepness and depth of everything. Could he climb the Fang with one bad foot? Could anyone climb it?

Footsteps pounded up the stairs.

"Todd? This math problem is driving me insane. Can you give me a hand?"

"Why pick on me, Jess? You always get better marks."

Todd hurriedly folded the stereo glasses and stuffed the air photos into the cupboard. For some reason he didn't want Jess to catch him looking at the photos.

As he analyzed the math problem, Todd felt an unexpected rush of confidence. "This problem is

dead simple, Jess, as long as you go step by step.
The trouble is, you're trying to rush through it."

Later that night Todd dreamed he was climbing
the Witch's Fang. The dream seemed to go on
forever. Sweat was pouring down his face as he
dragged himself over the crumbling rocks. It was
growing steadily hotter. Steam or smoke, he couldn't
tell which, was swirling around his legs and dragging him back. He stumbled and fell. The rocks
around him melted and shot upward in an arc of
flame, and Todd felt himself tumbling end over end
into the blackened chasm below.

Was he awake? Todd peered into the darkness.
Then he was climbing the Fang again, only this
time the air was bitterly cold. He zipped up his
anorak, but couldn't find any mitts. His hands
were freezing, and the breath from his nostrils was
turning into hoarfrost. When he clutched a rock for
support, his fingers stuck fast. He struggled to rip
them loose. Glancing upwards, he saw the Fang
glistening like a sharp, deadly icicle. The ice gripping his fingers crept down his arms, across his
shoulders, through his ribs, searching for the heart.

Todd awoke with a start. At least he hoped he
was awake this time. He rolled out of bed and
shuffled into the bathroom. The face staring back
at him from the mirror, though undoubtedly his
own, looked pale and haggard. Oh well, there was
nothing like the sound of a flushing toilet to bring
a person down to earth.

Back in bed Todd struggled to keep the nightmare thoughts at bay. Finally he flicked on the light, opened a recent issue of *Scientific American* and turned to an article about quasars. Think quasars. And that way he finally did manage to fall asleep.

When Todd stumbled into the kitchen next morning, Jess was already downing her usual granola, applesauce and yogurt. No toast dripping with butter and jam, or bacon and fried eggs laced with ketchup for her.

"Have you ever seen a ballet dancer with fat legs?" Jess was always asking him.

Of course he hadn't. But how she could dance her way through life on so little food was a miracle. Todd dug into his oatmeal porridge while bacon and eggs spluttered in the frying pan. He patted his long, skinny legs. No worry about excess fat there.

Todd glanced at Jess. Should he say anything about his newly hatched plan? Was this even the right word? he wondered. Didn't planning mean you sat down, looked at the problem, maybe drew up a list of the pros and cons before deciding on a course of action? All he'd done was lie awake half the night, tossing and turning and fighting off nightmares. When the alarm finally went off, this crazy scheme — plan, call it what you want — was firmly camped on his bed, worrying the last shreds of sleep and eventually forcing him to get up.

Why should he talk to his sister? Either she would ridicule the idea and laugh that grating laugh of hers, or she'd try to take over. No, darn it all, this was his idea. Besides, his parents had just come into the kitchen and turned on the radio. With the news and weather drowning out everything else, sensible talk was impossible: "A massive high-pressure system currently offshore is dominating all of coastal British Columbia."

After her morning weather fix, Norma Rushton relaxed and took a sip of coffee.

"God's in his heaven and all's right with the weather, if not the world," Sam announced from behind his morning newspaper.

Jess stretched and stood up.

"Are you meeting Howie at lunch?" Todd asked.

"Of course. I always meet Howie for lunch. Why are you asking?"

"No particular reason. I need to talk to him."

"About what?"

"It's none of your business, Jess."

"Suit yourself."

She was staring at him, obviously curious. Good. Todd gulped down the sense of relief that broke against his lungs like rarefied mountain air. He had crossed the first major crevasse. Although Howie didn't know it yet, although the scheme was still simmering in his own head, somehow the two of them were going to climb the Witch's Fang. And he would break the news at lunch.

✧ CHAPTER 2

AT LUNCHTIME TODD HURRIED DOWN to the lower soccer field. Jess and Howie were already there, sitting on a bench with their backs towards him. Howie had one arm draped over Jess's shoulder. Typical. Ever since they had been in Grade Six, Howie had been devoted to Jess. It didn't matter that the other guys teased him or that Jess's feelings were ambivalent — nothing seemed to faze Howie, star of the soccer team, most popular kid around.

Todd clapped him on the shoulder. "How's everything?"

"Would have been better without this morning's chemistry test," Howie replied, biting a chunk from his apple.

Jess was eyeing him. "So what do you want, Todd?"

"I, uh, need to talk to you, Howie."

"No time like the present."

"I mean alone, Howie."

Howie pulled his cap over his eyes and took a furtive look around. "No prob. I think we're alone."

"Um, I mean just you, Howie."

Finally. "Oh, I get it. You want to talk to me without your sister around."

"Yeah, I suppose."

"What do you say, Jess?"

"Fine with me. Besides, I've got some math to finish." Jess kissed Howie lightly on the forehead and turned away.

"See you this eve, Jess?" Howie asked.

"Can't. I have ballet practice at six-thirty. Our annual show's coming up in May."

"How be I come over later and we watch the news with your dad? I see you, and we get informed at the same time."

Jess laughed. "What sacrifices you make for me, Howie."

Talk about three being a crowd, Todd thought. "Look, if I'm interrupting ..."

"No, I'm just leaving. See you later this evening, Howie."

"Sure." Howie folded his arms across his chest. "Well?"

"Todd sat down beside him. "I think we should try to climb the Witch's Fang," he heard himself saying.

No reply from Howie.

"You know, sometime this spring. It's the perfect time of year."

Howie went on crunching his apple.

"Can't you get rid of that revolting apple and say something, Howie?"

Howie shot the core into space. "How's the foot these days?"

"If you're suggesting I'm in no shape for climbing the Fang, why not say so."

"It's been how long since you've climbed anything serious?"

"Not since last spring, before my accident. But listen, Howie, I have almost two months to get in shape, assuming we climb the Fang on the May long weekend."

"Why the Witch's Fang right now? There are easier mountains around."

Todd shook his head. How could he explain what he himself scarcely understood. He was in no mood to analyse his feelings, least of all in Howie's presence. But Howie was waiting for an answer, arms folded over his chest.

"There may be several groups going after the Witch's Fang this year. Even as a kid I dreamed I'd be the first to climb it.

"Is that all?"

"Maybe not, Howie. But it's what finally made up my mind for me."

"Climbing the Witch's Fang — I dunno, it seems far-fetched."

"I want to, Howie."

"And you think you're up to it?"

"If I don't give it a try, how will I ever know?"

Howie gave him a shove and tried to wrestle him off the bench. "Wow, there's strength in those muscles yet. And you're sounding more like my old friend instead of the wizened-up character of the past few months."

"Wizened?"

"Yeah, shrivelled up like an old sausage. Slouching around with your chin on your chest and a chip on your shoulder, not bothering to talk to your best friend."

"Have I been that bad, Howie?"

"Terrible."

"Sorry, I didn't realize."

"Don't be sorry. Be mad, be a jerk, but welcome back to the land of the living."

"Why didn't you tell me?"

"You think I didn't try? How many times have I suggested we take in a show together, watch a video ...?"

"And I'm always too busy with physio or swimming or ..."

"Yeah."

"But the question remains — will you come, Howie?"

"If you feel up to it, no prob. Must be almost a year since we climbed together. Remember the new route we did on Zodiac Wall — wasn't that the ultimate? Talk about gut-wrenching exposure. You could see through your feet a hundred metres straight to the ground. Yeah, it would be great to have a go at the Fang. One condition, though — "

"What's that, Howie?"

"That we ask Jess to come along."

"Why her? Why not us two? Listen, Howie, it'll go that much slower with three to a rope, plus increase the danger from rockfall."

"Granted, but it will also be safer. Remember this mountain isn't a piece of cake. It's one tough climb. If anyone gets hurt, at least two able bodies are left."

"We could ask somebody else."

"Can you think of anyone better than Jess?"

"Not really." And if they started asking around, word would leak out they were set to climb the Fang and his dad would veto the trip as being too dangerous or something. He didn't want to take that risk. "You just can't leave her behind, can you?"

Howie grinned. "We'll appoint her as expedition cook. Take it or leave it."

"Cook? You know what will happen? She'll poison us with her tuna-and-noodle casserole."

Todd laughed, but it wasn't funny. Already he could picture them shutting him out — two versus one. Take it or leave it — and that stupid grin on Howie's face.

"I'll skip soccer after school and we'll meet at your place before Jess heads off to ballet. How's that?" Howie asked.

"Sure, fine — anything you want, Howie."

Todd lingered behind, watching a guy kicking a soccer ball into the air. The ground was still too wet, and each time the ball rebounded with a watery splat.

Am I crazy? Todd wondered. Why was he deliberately walking into the path of pain? Because there was no use kidding himself — climbing the Witch's Fang, if indeed he could climb it, would be a painful haul.

Over the past year he'd certainly had enough pain. But on the morning of the accident itself, he had felt great. As he looked back everything seemed so ordinary — no tilting of the world, no sense of doom, no omens.

He remembered opening the car window and the rush of air. The scent of balsam poplars and damp undergrowth from the river nearby was overpowering. The chortling of red-winged blackbirds almost drowned out the car stereo. The sun bit the pavement and danced in dreams over the next hill and the next. The day promised to be a scorcher.

A swim in the lake, followed by a cold drink at his friend's place — that would sure hit the spot. The muscles in his arms, shoulders and neck, stiff from tree planting, and now several hours of steady driving, were clamouring for a stretch. Half an hour and he'd be there …

Like a sailing ship on an aimless tack, Todd's car drifted across the centre line. The driver of the oncoming vehicle leaned against her horn. Still

Todd didn't wake up. Seconds later the cars sideswiped each other, spun out of control and came to rest in the ditch. A woman's scream broke the silence.

Todd's fingers reached automatically for the door. It wasn't there. Nothing was in its proper place any more, and that included him.

The shaft of the steering column lay twisted across the driver's seat, blocking what remained of the door. Todd tried to wrestle it away. His hands were bleeding. For an instant he sank back on the seat, exhausted. The smell of gear oil, gas and his own blood was flowing over him, threatening to suffocate him.

"The other door then ..." Todd pressed his shoulders against the scarred metal. Something was holding him back. His fingers fumbled at the seat belt until it fell loose. Go now, he told himself. What was wrong? Why couldn't he pull his blasted leg free?

"Help!" Todd heard himself pleading in an old man's voice. "Get me out. It'll go up. I'll burn."

When a passing truck driver finally pulled his leg free from the wreckage, the pain struck. Not the play pain of cuts and bruises and running to Mommy or Daddy for a bandage, but pain plucking him apart with giant pincers, then collapsing him like a spent flower.

"No more," he begged.

But they dragged him across the rough gravel of the shoulder, away from the scorched steel and

stinking pools of oil. Unbelievably he didn't pass
out ...

When Todd arrived home after school, the tape
deck was already going.

"Not more ballet music!"

Jess and Howie were sitting side by side at the
kitchen table, talking and stuffing themselves
with the chocolate brownies he had planned for
supper. They didn't notice his entrance.

"I thought you two would have the maps and air
photos all spread out," Todd complained.

"No way! This is your climb, Todd. I haven't
spoken to Jess about it."

"Spoken to me about what?" Jess demanded.

Great! Todd thought. He leaves me to ask her.

"About the Witch's Fang," he replied wearily.
"We want to climb it this spring. Howie thinks you
should come."

Jess hesitated. "What do you think, Todd?"

"Well, I'm asking you, aren't I?"

"Sort of."

"All you need to say is yes or no, I do or I don't
want to come."

"Let me think about it for a minute. For sure I
couldn't go until after my ballet performance."

"When's that?"

"Friday evening of the May long weekend."

Todd checked his calendar. In spite of the long
weekend coming early this year, it was awfully

close to when the Seattle Mountaineers were planning their trip.

"I wouldn't mind coming," Jess said. "I mean, it
is the last unclimbed peak left near Vancouver."

"Which is not the only reason for going, Jess."

"Oh? You could have fooled me. How come you
decided to go the moment Dad announced the
Seattle Mountaineers were interested?"

"I hope you had your tape recorder going when
you were eavesdropping on Dad and me, Jess,
because it so happens you're wrong."

Howie jumped in. "There'd be no problem leaving early Saturday morning after Jess's show,
would there, Todd?"

"I suppose not," Todd found himself saying.
"We'd still have three days."

"We want you along, Jess."

"I'm not so sure Todd does."

"Do I have to put it in writing, Jess?"

"So it's all settled," Howie told them. "We leave
early Saturday morning of the May long weekend.
Let's drag out those maps now."

"I'll join you two when I've finished my math
homework," Jess said.

Upstairs, surrounded by air photos, maps and
a few faded photographs from Sam's collection,
Todd began to relax. It was like sifting through the
pages of a well-loved book. With luck they should
have an hour or so of peace before his parents
arrived home. Todd watched silently as Howie
studied the air photos and the map with Sam's

pencilled-in approach route. At last Howie lifted his head from the stereo glasses.

"Climbable, I guess."

"Is that all you've got to say, Howie?"

"What should I say?"

"I don't know. Elaborate."

"No prob. What we have here is a steep tower, equally impressive-looking from all sides, even allowing for the usual air-photo exaggeration. The south ridge would make an interesting climb ... How am I doing?"

"Great, Howie. Vintage mountaineering description. Go on."

Howie leafed through a couple of old Canadian Alpine Club journals, then bent over the stereo glasses again.

"So?"

"The Fang looks as radical as anything we've ever tackled — including our winter climb of Mt. Slesse. Hey, do you remember that disintegrating ice near the top, how it was sloughing off under our crampons as the warm front moved in?"

"I can still hear the sound. I also remember saying my prayers."

"Extreme, all right. You know, my old man thinks climbers are crazy. I tell him driving is more dangerous. I tell him about your accident and he still shakes his head. When he's into serious drinking, he goes all weepy, says I'll kill myself and leave him a lonely old man."

"Jeez, Howie, I knew it was bad."

"He's worse since Mom left. Sometimes I swear the whole apartment stinks of booze, and I have to escape for fresh air. If it wasn't for your place ..." Howie boxed Todd on the shoulder. "You know, I'm really looking forward to this climb, three whole days away, just you and Jess and me, nobody to bother us. Which reminds me — one possible problem."

"What's that?"

"I just want to get one thing clear — if this turns into a race for the summit, count me out."

"Nobody mentioned a race."

"Because I don't need to climb this particular rock heap and I don't want to get mixed up in someone else's ego trip."

"Not to worry, Howie. All we have to do is keep quiet and make sure Kurt doesn't get wind of our plans."

"Kurt may not be the only problem. What's this business Jess mentioned about the Seattle Mountaineers?"

"Jess knows nothing. She's always barging into my business. Dad and I were discussing a letter from the Seattle Mountaineers, Jess overheard and suddenly she knows more than anyone else. They have no definite date, no definite plans, no definite anything except my sister's imagination."

"Okay, okay. So long as my position is clear."

Jess was coming up the stairs. Good, Todd thought. Anything to distract Howie.

"You should check out the geology of the Witch's

Fang area," Todd went on. "Some of the volcanoes actually broke through the ice sheets of the Pleistocene. Probably the Fang was one of them. If you'd been standing there, you would have seen molten lava pouring through the ice, steam billowing up, huge ice walls collapsing, fire and ice battling it out." Todd stopped. Instead of distracting Howie, he'd got carried away by his own enthusiasm.

"Jess, you'd better not back out," Howie was saying. "I need the company of another rational being on this trip."

"My brother is like this occasionally. I think he's harmless."

Darn it all, they were laughing at him.

"Back to business," Howie said suddenly. "Your folks will be home anytime and there's lots to discuss, including how we're going to schedule some climbing practice between now and May."

"Count me out," Jess said. "I'll be too busy practising for my show."

"I don't worry about you being out of shape," Howie assured her. "What I worry about is these two big louts here."

"What about equipment?" Todd asked, interrupting their dialogue.

"I'll bring my two ropes and climbing hardware," Howie volunteered. "And I guess three can fit into your tent, Todd, if we wedge Jess in the middle."

"We'll settle that later," she retorted. "Are you

taking any of your fancy climbing equipment, Howie?"

"Apart from the basics, I doubt it. What I've heard about the loose rock makes me think we'll be climbing on straight adrenaline and not much else."

There was the sound of a car driving up the back alley and stopping behind the house.

"It's them," Todd warned. "You better go, Howie, or Dad will start talking about climbing and you'll end up telling him we're planning to climb the Witch's Fang. I know he'd veto the trip. We need to keep this strictly to ourselves. Okay?"

"But I like talking to your dad. He's great, especially when he gets going about climbing."

"That's because you don't have to listen to him every day, Howie. Now go."

"Wait, we haven't discussed the most important part — food."

"We can do that some other time. We'll bring everything except for your snacks and lunches." Todd was propelling him towards the stairs.

"But not your bacon-rice-tomato mixture, please, Jess. It almost killed me last summer."

"You don't mean my delicious BRT?" Jess protested. "There was nothing wrong with it except the bacon was a bit green after riding around in my pack for a week."

"Spare me the gruesome details."

"What about a car?" Todd asked. "Can you get your old man's?"

"Probably. I'll ask him closer to the time. If I know him, he'll be glued to the TV set all weekend. And as long as I don't mention that I need the car for a climbing trip, there'll be no questions asked."

"Different from this house. But be super careful when you broach the subject, Howie. We need that car."

"No prob, I know how to approach him." He hesitated at the door. "Are we still going to watch the news with your dad, Jess?"

"Let's skip it for tonight, Howie. I'll be tired after ballet."

"Yeah, you're right — not that I'm happy."

Todd was still folding the maps when his parents came in.

"Planning a trip?" Sam asked.

"Possibly." Better to sound noncommittal.

"I hope Howie is going with you. He's a good, steady climber. I collided with him on the front steps, by the way. Big fellow, that."

"He's been big for years. Haven't you noticed?" Todd mumbled as he stuffed the maps away.

"You've got them the wrong way around, Todd. The map title should be at the top. Never mind, I'll do it."

If you weren't always watching over my shoulder, I'd get it right, Todd thought.

"I see you have the Garibaldi area maps out. There's an Alpine Club ski trip going there next weekend. Are you interested?"

"I doubt it. I may try some rock climbing. If Jess and Howie and I are planning a trip for later on, I need to get in shape."

"Good. I'm glad you're a party of three. It's always safer to travel with more than two, especially on a glacier. Personally, I can't understand this solo mountaineering business, or the sudden craze for climbing without ropes or protection of any kind."

Sam was into lecturing. Todd wasn't listening. They were going, they were actually going to climb the Witch's Fang. Nothing else mattered.

"There have been a number of completely unnecessary accidents in the club recently: climbers neglecting to rope up on glaciers, trusting old fixed ropes and pins, rapelling unsafely." Sam droned on and on.

Too bad about the Seattle Mountaineers. Who cared about Kurt or anyone else? Jess and Howie were coming with him, of course, but even they were incidental. This was his plan, his trip. There was only the Fang rising above the snow fields like a shimmering beacon and he, Todd Rushton, careening towards it.

✧ CHAPTER 3

TODD SAT DOWN AND LEANED against the sun-warmed wall. They had chosen this particular location for their climbing exercise because the wall faced west and lapped up the last traces of afternoon sun. Todd patted the rough surface. It was perfect for "buildering" — lots of toeholds, but small and far enough apart to be challenging. It helped that the wall was removed from any major thoroughfares, car or pedestrian. And exam time at the university meant that fewer students were up and about. No point in being exhibitionists, especially now that the campus security force was cracking down on climbers. Todd chuckled to himself. Not so long ago two of their club members had been caught buildering in a shopping mall on the same evening as a jewellery store break-in. As prime suspects they had spent the rest of the night in jail.

Buildering had certainly caught on over the

past few years. In some places, special climbing walls had been built inside, and whole families were taking up the sport. If you didn't have the time or inclination to head for the local hills, you could find a handy wall somewhere in town. And for some the activity had become an end in itself. Climbing with all the newest gear, hands coated with chalk dust to improve their grip, these enthusiasts rarely ventured into the real mountains.

"Addicts," Sam complained in his most conservative tone. "And they even race each other up and down the walls."

But not Todd. If he wasn't dreaming of Yosemite or the grey, looming walls of the Squamish Chief, his vision was focused on the range after range of glaciated peaks stretching north and west from Vancouver to Alaska. In those mountains were unclimbed north faces as challenging as the legendary ones of Europe, and areas virtually untouched by climbers. Todd sighed. Somehow he had to find his way back into that world.

What was keeping Howie? He'd better come soon or they'd lose their sun. Already it was creeping up the wall and leaving him in shade.

Todd pulled his rubber-soled climbing shoes from his pack. Last spring he had bought them second-hand, in anticipation of a great climbing season. A perfect fit back then, but never used since the car accident. Todd struggled with the left shoe. After pulling out the lace, he managed to squeeze his foot inside, but tying it up was another matter. The foot looked like a misshapen parcel when he was finished. And he was planning to climb with that?

Just then Howie arrived.

"Sorry for being late. My old man was in such bad shape I had trouble getting away. No sign of the campus cops?"

"Not yet. Listen, it's no use, Howie. I can't climb with this." Todd lifted his left foot as if it was some mummified object from a display case.

Howie stared at it for a moment. "It's a bit gross-looking, granted. But you'll manage. People climb without toes, without their real feet, without legs, even. Come on, let's set the rope up."

They made their way to the third floor of the building and onto a flat roof where they dumped their packs. Howie broke a giant chocolate-chip cookie in two and gave half to Todd.

"Come on, eat. Look at your wasted little calf muscles. They need food and exercise."

It was a perfect place for a practice session — a flat roof, slightly elevated around the edge, with several ventilation ducts that not only hid them from view but also served as anchors for the rope. Howie placed slings around two side-by-side vents, took a couple of oblong metal rings from his pack, attached these carabiners to the slings and then into a figure-eight knot on the main climbing rope. Todd watched his methodical movements. Howie was never a person to sacrifice safety for speed.

"You ready?" Howie asked finally.

"Me?"

"Yeah, you, Todd. We're doing this exercise for your sake, remember? Not that I'm unhappy to be here. My old man was out to make life miserable for me this afternoon."

Of course Howie was there because of him. Todd rummaged through the pile of equipment and found his climbing harness. When had he last used it? He must have been in a big hurry, judging by the tangled nylon straps.

"I'll give you a hand," Howie said, starting to sort through the straps.

"I can do it myself."

"Suit yourself."

Todd stepped into the loops, pulled them high up on his legs, then fastened the strap around his waist. As he fumbled with the carabiner, the metal ring slipped through his fingers, bounced off the edge of the roof and disappeared.

"Hope nobody was below."

"Never mind, I've got another 'biner," Howie told him. "And you can use my descender for going down."

"Another piece of gadgetry," Sam had snorted when Howie showed up with his newest descender.

"Think of it as a superior carabiner, a sort of built-in friction maker," Howie had explained. "Instead of wrapping your rappel rope around the 'biner, you simply slip it through the hole in the descender, then loop it around."

"Safer and more reliable than the old method of

sliding down a rope," Sam finally had to admit.

Howie handed Todd the descender and patted him on the shoulder. "Think of me relaxing up here in the sunshine while you're struggling down below."

"As long as you stay awake while you're belaying me, I don't care."

Todd lifted the climbing rope and walked to the edge of the roof. He'd better not drop Howie's descender. After looping his rappel rope through it and checking that everything was properly attached to his climbing harness, he let the end of the rope slip over the edge.

"All clear," he told Howie.

"Go, man."

With one hand grasping the rappel rope above the descender and the other holding lower down, Todd stepped backward off the roof. He must have rappelled hundreds of times, but not within the past year, and now excitement was gripping him as it had on that first rappel many years ago.

He could hear the long-ago voice of his father guiding him down the Lighthouse Park cliffs. The air had been cool and clear then too. Twenty-five metres straight below him, the sea had washed over the rocks, pushing and pulling relentlessly at the long kelp strands.

"Keep watching me as you go over the edge, Todd. Don't look down."

"But, Dad, there's an overhang."

"No, it's just steep. Don't worry, I've got you on a safety line."

"Are you holding me real tight?"

"You bet. But don't hug the rock. Lean back, Todd, feet wide apart. That's the way — tap-dance down."

"It's kind of fun, Dad."

"Of course it's fun."

Dance. Dance. Nothing to it. Todd's left foot landed hard against the pavement. Pain that he had forgotten for the moment returned with a sharp jab.

Howie peered over the roof. "Everything under control?"

"Apart from landing too hard, yes."

Todd unwound the rappel rope from the descender, tied the end in a figure-eight knot, attached it to his climbing harness and then flicked the rope a couple of times. "You can take up the slack, Howie." A moment later he felt a sharp jerk on his harness.

"Got you on belay," Howie called. "I'd recommend you come pronto. The climate up here is great."

Already the sun had moved halfway up the wall. The stark contrast between light and shade had erased the small indentations, making the wall appear more formidable. And to think that only a year ago, he had climbed it without any rope or aid on a friend's bet. Of course, he hadn't breathed a word to Sam — that would have produced an instant lecture on the hazards of new-style climbing. What had surprised him, though, was Howie's reaction or lack thereof. "People do what they have to," he said, shrugging. No congratulations, no pats on the back, no rehashing of the dicey sections — nothing.

The rope flicked against his harness again. "You coming?" Howie called.

"Sure. Keep your shirt on," Todd muttered.

He took a few deep breaths and swung his arms over his head in an effort to relax. This whole exercise was feeling too much like exams. The first move was obvious — an angular rock jutting from the concrete — the perfect toehold. Todd eased his left foot up, at the same time pressing down hard on the ridged surface with his outstretched fingers. The bad ankle wobbled from the tension, but there was no real pain, not yet.

"Go easy," he told himself. "Let it glide. Don't start thrashing around for handholds." Like most climbers on a tough pitch, Todd kept up a running commentary, not all of it repeatable.

"What's going on down there?" Howie was draped over the roof edge like a waiting vulture.

"Give me some slack, Howie. I can hardly breathe."

The rope leading down to his climbing harness relaxed, but Howie's ever-present voice was relentless. "Couple of good holds above you. No, farther to the right. Yeah, that's it. Now up. Shout if you want more slack."

"Give me a break, will you, Howie?"

Todd continued to climb and resumed his running commentary: "Press down with both arms, spread-eagle the legs and hold that tension. Now slide the bad foot up ... slowly, slowly." Jab of pain there. He couldn't hold himself indefinitely on his arms. Calf muscles going jittery. "Come on, up you go."

Todd eased himself onto a window ledge using one knee, a practice frowned on by climbing purists, but often handy. Time for a break. His left foot was beginning to throb from the continuous pressure.

"Time out, Howie, I'd like to give my foot a rest. Can you tighten up the rope?"

"Roger. I'll keep you on belay. No hurry — I'm enjoying the sunshine here."

Todd stood up on the ledge and leaned back until the rope was taking his full weight. What a relief! He let himself sway back and forth in front of the window, doing a pantomime of a window washer. Too bad there were no students inside to appreciate his great show.

Todd wiped the sweat from his hands. Nerves or the unaccustomed physical exertion? Whatever, it was time for some chalk. He reached into his chalk bag and rubbed the white stuff over his palms. There, that should keep his hands from slipping for a while. He watched the cloud of chalk dust drifting down, down ... Hello, there were two students standing below, watching him.

"Campus cop next block over," they warned.

Howie's face reappeared, this time looking concerned. "You can use the rope to climb up, or I can lower you down. Just hurry it up."

"You'll have to give me a few more minutes. I want to finish the climb myself."

"Whatever, but move. I don't want to be caught holding the rope, so to speak."

Something in Howie's voice reminded him of his father. Once, a long time ago, he remembered Sam's having to drag him up a rock face. He had been working his way up a crack, jamming his arms and feet in for leverage and doing just fine until the crack flared into a full-blown chimney.

"Feet against one side, back against the other and wedge yourself up," Sam told him.

"The chimney is too wide, Dad. My legs won't reach across."

After Sam had dragged him up, he burst into tears, and nothing his father tried to say or do could stop the flow.

Well, Howie had better relax. No matter what, he intended to finish this climb on his own.

"Climbing," Todd called up.

"Let's see some action, then," was the reply.

Todd glided his good foot onto a toe-hold slightly above the window ledge. He looked everywhere for another substantial hold. There was nothing within reach, and squinting his eyes against the intense sunlight only increased the sensation of smoothness.

Now activate the left foot. He had to keep moving — give the muscles time to protest and it was all over. There was a small indentation half a metre away — nothing in between, except friction holds. What he needed here was glue, not chalk. Both legs were shaking, and his arms too, like leaves in the wind.

"Listen, Howie, you better be holding that rope, because I'm about to peel off."

Todd's fingers slipped, caressing the surface of the wall for an instant, then clutching at air. He fell, but only as far as the rope gave with his weight. Nobody could accuse him of not trying.

Howie's head jerked into sight again. Was it the angle that made his face look so contorted? He seemed to be gesturing, trying to say something. Todd glanced down and saw a campus security officer looking up.

"Oh no, it's the cops."

Howie tugged on the rope and called down quietly, "The other cop is on his way up, but he hasn't made it here yet. Hurry. Use the rope. I'm holding you."

Todd gripped the rope with both hands and,

bracing his legs against the wall, started to work his way up. By now the officer below was waving his arms and shouting, "Come down."

No way I'm going down, Todd thought. As Howie was helping him over the edge, another officer burst through the emergency exit onto the roof.

"Uh-oh," Howie said, "I think we're going to need some luck to squirm out of this one. Let me do the talking. I get lots of practice with my old man."

"You two fellows are looking at a stiff fine," the officer called out. "Since the accident here a month ago, we've been cracking down on illegal climbers."

"We're illegal?" Howie asked innocently.

"News of the accident was all over the newspapers," the officer snapped. "You fellows must be crazy, climbing vertical walls."

"We have a rope," Howie said.

"That's not the point. It's strictly illegal to climb university buildings. Last week we caught one fellow who looked like a plumber, he was lugging so much junk around."

"You mean climbing hardware?"

"I don't care what it was. This idiot was chipping at the wall with a hammer and pounding in nails — spikes, mind you, not little thumbtacks."

Howie was nodding. "Pitons are destructive, all right. Frankly I prefer these chocks." He produced a small metal knob with a length of wire attached.

The officer handled it cautiously. "I think you fellows are nuts."

"Handy little gadgets," Howie babbled on. "And definitely more environmentally friendly than pitons. Stuff this chock into a crack and you've got an instant belay or tie-in for your rope."

"Listen, I don't understand why you're climbing this wall, but I do know you're destroying this university, chip by chip. Your dollars are going up in dust."

"It's unconscionable," Howie agreed.

"All right, I'm not wasting any more breath on you fellows. There are forms to fill out and your parents to notify."

As Howie was bending over to pick up the rope, he whispered to Todd, "If he sends us ahead through the emergency exit, be prepared to make a break for it."

"But if we get caught, it'll only make matters worse, Howie."

"Worse? What's worse than being grounded for the next two months? No Jess, no climbing the Witch's Fang, no soccer."

"Come on, you two, make it snappy." The security officer nudged them towards the door.

Howie grinned. "As I suspected. When your feet hit the corridor, run!"

"Which way?"

"It doesn't matter. Just run." He pushed Todd over the door sill.

"Stop!" the security officer yelled.

Todd felt a sharp pain jolting through his foot when he hit the corridor. All very well for Howie to say run. Was the cop right behind? He glanced back and saw the officer flying over the door sill. A second later there was an unmistakable ripping sound as his jacket caught on the emergency-door lever.

"He'll be calling the other guy on his radio," Howie warned. "Come on, down these stairs." He grabbed Todd by the arm.

"Hold it. I can't go three steps at a time."

He hadn't run this fast since he was a kid stealing peaches from a neighbour's yard. One floor above them, but coming closer, were the pounding footsteps of the security officer.

"I can't keep up the pace," Todd gasped. "You go on."

"No way — we're in this together."

Howie wrenched open a door leading into the back alley and pushed Todd through. Luckily there were no security officers waiting to intercept them, and better still, the freight door leading into the nearby library was wide open. Once through, Howie swung the massive door shut and lifted the bar into lock position.

"That should hold them for a while."

There were angry voices and fists thumping on the door.

"Why don't we bivouac inside the library until they calm down?" Howie suggested.

"Brilliant idea, Howie. They won't find us in the crowds there."

Upstairs, the library was jammed with students cramming for exams. After stashing their packs and jackets in the cubicles outside, Howie and Todd drifted among the shelves, keeping an eye open for an empty desk and pretending to look for books. Twice a campus security officer wandered into the library, walked briefly around the room, then left.

"I knew we looked mature," Howie gloated. "Without our gear we blend perfectly into this high-class crowd."

Eventually a couple of students left for an early supper, and Todd and Howie grabbed the empty seats. Todd opened the book he had lifted from the shelves, *Wilderness First Aid*, and started reading.

Another security officer came in and strolled aimlessly down the rows, brushing the back of Todd's chair. Todd could feel the muscles at the back of his neck tightening. Boy, would he ever have liked to be out of there!

Howie poked him in the side. "Why don't we head home? It's after six-thirty and the coast should be clear. My old man will be half-starved by now."

Once they were outside in the cool evening air, waiting for the bus home, Todd began to relax. "I'm sorry you never had a turn on the wall, Howie. It felt great to be climbing again."

"Yeah, so great you couldn't speed things up even though the campus cops were around. You can't say we weren't warned."

"I wanted to finish the climb by myself, Howie."

"Sure, I know. But you get caught by the campus cops and what happens? A lecture from your dad about being a responsible self-disciplined young man, maybe a few extra chores around the house to make up for the fine, which they pay. Look at it from my perspective. The old man flies into a rage and I get grounded for the rest of the year and have to use my job money to pay the fine. Meanwhile, Jess probably forgets what I look like, if she even cares."

"If she even cares ... Of all the dumb things to say. Do you think Jess would be coming on the climbing trip if it was just me going?"

"I dunno. Maybe. And how would you know if Jess cares about me? Listening to you two talking, I get the impression you don't know much about each other."

"Well, we have eaten breakfast together for the past seventeen years."

Howie grinned. "That's a pile of granola and yogurt."

"Yeah, health food and ballet — Jess's obsessions."

"And your obsession is climbing the Witch's Fang, eh?"

"I wouldn't call it an obsession."

Todd stared out the bus window, watching the houses flick past. Sometimes it annoyed him how Howie changed the subject, became too personal, in the same way Jess did. Maybe they learned the habit from each other.

"So what would you call it?" Howie asked.

"I guess I'd say conditions are perfect for climbing the Fang, and time is, well, running out."

"Why worry? Spring comes next year at the same time, same place. The Witch's Fang isn't going to run away."

"But it's still unclimbed. By next year someone else may have climbed it. Doesn't that mean anything to you?"

Howie shook his head. "Just being in the mountains with you and Jess is good enough for me. The unclimbed bit is an added bonus — the chocolate after the dessert."

"So what's the trouble, Howie?"

"I can't shake off the notion that you're pushing it and after watching you today — "

"But I've got several more weekends for practising, Howie. If you don't think it's enough, I can do some workouts on the new climbing wall."

"If you weren't my old climbing buddy, I'd be tempted to drop the whole idea."

"Thanks, Howie."

"Don't thank me. I just helped you miss your bus stop. Come on, I'll walk back with you."

They got off the bus and walked the short distance to Todd's house.

"So next weekend it's the Smoke Bluffs, maybe the Squamish Rock the week after, and soon it'll be time for the real thing," Todd said when they reached his door.

"Sure," Howie repeated, "the real thing." He

stopped on the steps.

"Are you coming in or not?"

"Wish I could, Todd, but I'm already late. By the way, what are you telling your dad about our climbing trip?"

"I've been purposefully vague. All I told him was that you and Jess and I are planning some sort of trip."

"Better give it more thought. I don't like the idea of straight lying."

"You don't need to remind me, Howie."

"Say hi to Jess for me. Tell her I may not get around to calling her this eve."

"I heard from the Seattle Mountaineers again," Todd's father said later, sliding a letter across the kitchen table. "They are definitely coming to climb the Witch's Fang at the end of May."

Todd almost choked on his mashed potatoes. "Did they give an exact date?"

"I don't think so. But you can read the letter yourself. They also want to borrow my air photos."

They did? At the moment the air photos were sitting under some books on his desk.

"I'm wondering whether I should circulate their letter at our next Alpine Club meeting."

"No, don't. Kurt will find out. I mean, wouldn't it be better to sit on it for a while?"

Jess was staring at him from across the table. If she said anything and blew their plans ... Circumstances were conspiring against him, all right.

Maybe he should tell his father. And risk having him veto the trip because it was too dangerous, or they were too young to go alone, or the conditions weren't a hundred percent perfect? No way. This was his trip. And he wasn't about to share the Fang with a bunch of complete outsiders either.

"Suit yourself," Sam said finally, handing him the letter. "Do what you want with it. By the way, what have you planned for trips?"

"You keep asking me. As I already told you, I'm trying some rock climbing. Maybe later I'll go on a longer trip."

"But Jess and Howie would be going along?"

"Yes, Dad, I'm not going anywhere by myself."

"Good."

"Have you tried out your heavy climbing boots recently?" Norma asked. "If they don't fit, you could talk to your physiotherapist and possibly have a special boot made."

"I'm sure I could, Mother."

Todd speared another carrot on his fork. No matter what obstacles were thrown into his path, he was going to climb the Witch's Fang. Only seventy kilometres to the northwest, surrounded by silent snow fields, the peak was waiting for him.

But his mother was right about one thing: he should go downstairs after dinner and try out his climbing boots, maybe give them a new coat of waterproofing.

✧ CHAPTER 4

THE WEEKS BEFORE THE CLIMBING TRIP were full: there were several climbing sessions during which Todd's confidence began to return, hours spent over maps and air photos plotting routes up the Witch's Fang, the usual quota of family squabbles and crises ...

"Todd, I appreciate the fact that you're sick of the same tape. So am I. But I have to practise for next Friday's ballet performance."

"Do you have some of my maps and air photos, Todd?" His father hovered around him. "I noticed the ones covering the Witch's Fang area are missing."

"Not surprising — I'm doing a project on the volcanic areas of the coast."

The final week dragged by. Friday was the worst day, with everyone descending on him as he struggled to sort out last-minute food and gear.

"Todd, you'll have to move your junk from the kitchen counter. We're eating early because of my ballet performance tonight."

"So when did my equipment become junk?"

"Quit the lawyer jargon and move, Todd."

"Does the whole world have to roll over and play dead because of your ballet performance?"

"No, but the part of it on this kitchen counter better roll over. And fast," Norma interrupted.

There was no point arguing. Todd shoved his stuff into the corner.

Sam poked his head around the corner, testing the atmosphere. "Final preparations for your weekend trip, eh?"

Todd braced himself for the inevitable continuation.

"What area did you finally settle on?"

"We're planning to do an easy trip north of the Witch's Fang." Todd had rehearsed the answer so many times in the past few days that any guilt feelings had drained away. Besides, mentioning the name of the mountain made it feel less like a direct lie.

"On skis?" Sam asked.

"No, on foot. But we can always throw skis in at the last minute if snow conditions look iffy."

"Remember to leave us a trip plan, mentioning the access roads and approximate time of return," Sam went on. "And don't forget your avalanche beacons and shovels. With the mild, sunny weather predicted, there could be some avalanche danger."

"Don't worry, Dad."

"I can't help worrying. Your mother and I have climbed long enough to know the dangers involved in mountaineering. Besides, you're young. You can easily be carried away by your own enthusiasm."

"Dad, I've been climbing since I was five years old."

"Not nearly long enough," Sam grumbled. "Well, give the old lady my regards when you see her. If there's any mountain that demands respect, it's the Witch's Fang."

Strange. It wasn't like his father to refer to a mountain in such personal terms. For an instant Todd had a vision of that dark decaying tooth rising from the whiteness of the surrounding snow fields — the Witch's Fang, the old lady, the black widow. Why did those images persist? It had to be the tension of the past few days getting to him. Call it sheer exhaustion.

If it wasn't for Howie, he would have fallen asleep during the Friday-evening ballet performance.

"Look at her, Todd. Isn't she amazing?"Another jab to the ribs a few minutes later as his head was nodding. "Did you see her spin? With balance like that, no wonder she can climb." Howie sighed and was silent for two minutes.

After the performance Howie insisted on going backstage to present Jess with the bouquet of flowers that had been wilting on his lap. Todd only managed to drag him away by protesting, "Even if you don't need sleep, I do."

"I'll phone you at quarter to five in the morning," Howie promised.

"Better not. A phone call will wake the parents and start them worrying. I don't want them fussing around while we're trying to leave."

"You'll sleep through your alarm, Todd. You've done it before."

"All right, I'll set two alarms."

Todd lay awake listening to the first tentative drops of rain against the hall skylight. The tempo built up, filling the eavestroughs and sending a torrent down the drainpipe. Through his bedroom wall, he could hear frantic gurgles as the pipe tried to gulp down the deluge. The overflow drops signalled defeat — plip-plop, plip-plop — the sound varying with point of impact. No use trying to outguess the rhythm; the wind saw to that, sending sudden squalls against the thin wall that separated him from the outside world.

When sleep finally came in brief snatches, the rain and the wind still circled the edge of his dreams, pulling him back time and time again from the precipices of the Witch's Fang. At four-thirty he was already wide awake. Abandoning any idea of further sleep, he tiptoed across to Jess's room and shook her awake. She mumbled a few incoherent words and pulled the blankets around her head.

"Keep the noise down, Jess. We don't want to

wake Mom and Dad. I'll put the coffee on and check back in five minutes. You better be up."

Every time Todd moved a dish or opened the fridge door, the racket seemed deafening. As long as his parents' door stayed shut all was well. What he didn't need now was a long-winded goodbye, brimming over with "take care, drive carefully, watch for avalanches ..."

"I don't have any appetite for granola. It's too early," Jess complained. She wrapped two pieces of toast in foil and poured the leftover coffee into a thermos.

On the dot of five-thirty, Howie pulled up in his dad's old Ford. Todd intercepted him outside.

"Don't slam any doors."

He glanced upstairs. Good, no lights yet. Asleep or at least pretending to be asleep. In a last-minute twinge of guilt he scribbled a note and left it lying on the breakfast table: "Have a good weekend. See you Monday eve. Probably late. Don't worry. Todd."

Then he was outside again, lifting the gear and stuffing it into the trunk of Howie's car.

"You know the trunk is busted?"

"Like everything else about my old man's car. He isn't motivated to fix anything these days, and I haven't had time. Use the rope to tie it down."

As the car eased away, a light flashed on. Probably Sam or Norma slipping downstairs to pour a glass of orange juice. Couldn't bear the tension of lying awake in bed, thinking of all the things they ought to have said. What a relief to finally be en route! Todd yawned and stretched out on the back seat. With his head resting against the door and his legs climbing up the opposite window, he found a semi-comfortable position.

The streetlights were still on, reflecting off pavement dotted by a light drizzle. The airport meteorologist sure misplaced this little system, Todd thought. Any precipitation was supposed to have stayed on the north coast. And what was falling as rain in the city might be snow at the highest elevations, creating possible avalanche conditions. Just their luck after the good weather of the past few days. No doubt those same thoughts were swirling in Sam's head as he lay awake listening to them leave.

Suddenly Howie stood on the brakes, stalling the car and throwing Todd against the front seat.

"Hey, take it easy," Todd said.

"That traffic light materialized from nowhere," Howie apologized.

"There isn't a seatbelt back here, Howie. If you're planning on running any more red lights, let me drive."

"It wasn't Howie's fault," Jess insisted. "I asked him if he could fix the tape deck."

"Then it was your fault for bugging the driver."

"You sure got out of the wrong side of the bed this morning, Todd."

"Let's not start our trip this way," Howie broke in. "We're all a bit tired and cranky."

"Bit cranky," Jess grumbled.

"Listen, I almost ran a red light, but I didn't hit anyone or anything, and I promise I won't be a bad boy again. Does that satisfy you two?"

Howie restarted the engine and drove on.

There were few cars at this early hour, but you couldn't be too careful, Todd figured. Ever since the car accident, he'd felt nervous driving, doubly so if someone else was behind the wheel. After a while the muscles in his neck, arms and legs began to uncoil and relax again. An occasional car light beamed at them from the tunnel of trees in Stanley Park, and then they were on the Lion's Gate Bridge, swinging over the darkness of Burrard Inlet. Todd stirred himself sufficiently to look down. Far below, the red and green lights from a single small fishing boat heading into port winked back. And beyond the harbour, where the mountains began to converge on the Fraser Valley, the first hint of morning was streaking the sky. North, where they were heading, it was still dark.

"You're not too sleepy?" Todd asked.

"Nope, I'm fine," Howie replied. "I'll let you know if I feel tired. Have a snooze."

"Thanks, Howie."

Jess was already asleep, her head bobbing lightly against Howie's shoulder.

"You never know — maybe I'll decide to turn around while you're both sleeping and head south to Yosemite. Escape the rain, abandon my old man, forget final exams — everything. Become a full-time climbing bum."

"I can't imagine you doing that," Todd mumbled sleepily.

"Neither can I, actually, but sometimes I feel like it."

Several times Todd was on the verge of drifting off, but a muscle spasm always jerked him awake. Why couldn't he sleep now, after tossing half the night? It was ironic. Other times, when he needed to stay alert, sleep came only too easily. He tried to banish the thought of one particular other time.

Less than a year ago, he'd been lying out there beside the highway, waiting. No longer the invincible golden boy streaking past highway signs, flashing down the ski run, shifting balance on a thin rock flake, with little thought for the hundred-metre drop. Now, suddenly, that airy space mattered. Was it some perverse trick of his imagination that kept rerunning the same scene, or was it a new image of himself — this figure lying by the wayside?

"Ambulance will be along in a few minutes, sonny. Just hold on."

Of course he'd hold on. Was there an alternative — like not holding on?

The woman in the other car had finally stopped screaming. "She'll be fine," someone said. "All she has is a bruised knee and a smashed car. Wish I could say the same for the young chap here."

Minutes drifted into hours, or so it seemed.

Finally an ambulance attendant bent over him. "Sorry, guy. Regulations prevent us from carrying anything stronger than nitrous oxide. Take a whiff. It'll help some."

Laughing gas — the stuff doesn't live up to its name.

"You have a broken femur and a smashed foot. We're taking you to hospital right away. But before moving you, we need to cut away your pants and splint the leg. Don't worry, I'll go real easy."

"Don't move me. Please don't."

"I know, it hurts. We'll go as carefully as we can. But we have to get you into the ambulance."

Was there ever a highway so long? Finally they carried him into the hospital emergency and gave him the shot of morphine that made hanging on less strenuous.

As the orthopedic surgeon leaned over him, he heard a faraway name.

"Yeung. I'm Dr. Raymond Yeung."

"I tree-planted with a Wayne Yeung."

"That's my son," the doctor said. "Your left foot is badly crushed. The important thing now is to relieve the pressure on the nerves. After that we'll see what happens."

Todd could hardly hear the doctor's voice any more, and although the light above him was brilliant, he was cold and shivering.

"Thanks for turning on the light, Jess," Howie said

as he geared the car down and turned left onto a logging road. "I think we have the right road, but I'd like to check with Todd."

"Shall I wake him?"

"Don't worry," Todd said. "I've been awake for ages. Where are we exactly?"

Howie handed him the map. "We're at the turnoff, I think. You're the expert — you better say."

Todd wiped the window and peered into the mist. There was the shack with the caved-in shake roof and above it a hand-lettered sign reading California Café. Who could forget that sign?

"You have to take the right fork, Howie — the one saying Turbid Creek — Main Line."

Howie gunned the car, throwing Todd against the back seat. "If I don't give her lots of gas on steep sections, she stalls," he explained. "And yes, I know, there's no seat belt back there."

"You really think we can coax this wreck to six hundred metres plus, Howie?"

"No prob."

Todd opened the window a crack. Rotten weather for starting a trip, but it was supposed to be good for the next two days. With some luck they might break loose from the fog higher up.

"Do you see any fresh tire tracks, Jess?"

"Everywhere."

"But not from this morning?"

"I'd have to get out and check. But don't lose any sleep over it, Todd. As the sign below said, there's active logging going on around here."

Easy for Jess to say. She had so little invested in the trip. Apart from getting up a few hours earlier and putting on her fancy new climbing gear, she had little else to do. Maps, air photos, food, emergency first aid — he'd taken care of the lot. But what if the Seattle Mountaineers had advanced their trip date as Sam had hinted? Then there was Kurt — the unknown element. If Sam had talked about the Mountaineers' letter once too often, Kurt might well be on his way here too.

Todd unzipped his pack and dragged out the 1:50000 map of the Witch's Fang. By now he knew the route almost by heart. Running his finger towards the peak, he became entangled in the circular contour lines: 1700 metres, 1850, 1900. Somewhere between 1950 and 2500 metres where the contours collapsed together into cliffs, his finger hesitated. With his nail he traced the lines. Round and round they swirled, dragging him to the very tip of the ancient volcano. He could hear his boots scrabbling against the rock, feel his fingernails scratching ...

Todd leaned out the car window, suddenly feeling queasy. Although he wasn't in a position to appreciate the fact, they were now above the fog.

"If you like, I'll stop the car and you can get out and take a stroll around," Howie suggested.

"No, we should keep going. I think the fresh air is helping some."

"No one in our family can read in cars," Jess

reminded him.

Another switchback. How many more could he survive? They must have been nearing the end of the road and the log landing where the felled trees were dragged from the woods.

Howie was bent over the wheel, coaxing the old wreck along. Snow in the middle of the road and water streaking down the rutted tracks would soon force them to stop.

"Last switchback," Howie called out. "Yee-ha!"

Todd stepped onto the empty log landing, stretched and took a deep breath. They were in luck — no sign of people or cars. He could feel the adrenaline build-up draining away. The sun felt warm and soothing on his skin. This world they had broken into, this hidden world of sun and meltwater and floating peaks, belonged to them alone. Across the valley, Mt. Garibaldi and the Black Tusk and range upon range of mountains loomed over the fog.

"Looks as if we've beaten everybody else," Jess remarked.

"Beaten who, Jess?"

"The Mountaineers, of course, or whoever else you thought might be here."

The word beaten seemed foreign in these surroundings, where humans were outsiders. But would Jess have said the word if the feeling hadn't shown on his face?

"Yee-ha!" The echo of Howie's mountain cry rose and stirred the Witch's Fang.

Todd shivered. In spite of the sunshine the air was surprisingly cool. It was time to get moving.

"We'll see the Fang only from higher up," he told the other two. "First off we'd better check our altitude." Todd pulled out Sam's old altimeter which he had hanging from a leather cord around his neck. "Hmm, seven hundred metres. The map shows us as higher — which means the barometer is on the rise and we may have a decent day tomorrow."

After divvying up the food and waiting while Howie sorted through his climbing hardware, they shouldered their packs and plunged into the usual logging mess: shattered tree trunks, twisted branches that caught in bootlaces, rusted sections of cable, discarded oil cans. Here and there patches of old snow that looked deceptively firm dropped them into deep holes. Progress was slow; conversation trailed off.

Todd found himself going over the worries of the past few days. Would his foot take this intense beating? You couldn't compare what he was doing now to a few leisurely afternoons of rock scrambling. And not telling Sam their exact destination? Understandable, given the circumstances, but that shouldn't have prevented him from telling someone else the details. If anything went wrong, they could rot away here forever. "Climbers missing. Destination unknown," Todd imagined the headlines saying. Simply put, he hadn't used his head.

Underfoot the slope was steepening. It was a

relief to leave the logged-off area — one more blown-down tree to straddle before they were in old growth forest. As they moved higher, the snow became continuous and the going easier, until they reached a band of cliffs.

"Rest stop!" Howie called." I need it even if you two don't. Why does my pack always seem twice as big as everyone else's?" He flopped down, letting his head rest against the top of his enormous pack, until the others caught up.

"Because you're carrying the ropes and more than half the climbing gear," Jess reminded him, "plus all your heavy army-surplus clothing."

"I need a rich great-uncle," Howie sighed. "And you know what I'll ask him for, Jess? Gore-Tex jacket and overpants — breathable, like the ads say, and underwear that wicks away the sweat and doesn't itch. New overmitts and a fancy pair of goggles would also be nice. And seeing as my feet are already damp, how about a pair of new climbing boots?"

"And nobody would recognize you," Jess said, "because you wouldn't look like an abominable snowman any more."

"I am kind of attached to my old woollies," Howie admitted. "What I really covet is a pair of your dad's old ski pants — the ones with the neat leather straps at the bottom that you can attach to your boots or push up under your knees, like Todd is wearing. Aren't they cute? I mean the ski pants, not Todd's knees."

"Thanks for the compliment, Howie. Maybe Dad could will you his second pair."

Todd had spread the map over his pack and was tracing a line with his finger. "According to the contours, we should traverse below the main cliffs on this diagonal shelf. Go too high and we're in trouble."

Howie tossed a few cashews and raisins in his mouth before handing the bag to Todd. "Have some gorp before we head on. You haven't eaten a thing."

Todd looked into the bag. "Picking out the cashews again, eh Howie?"

Howie grinned. "I left the prunes for you, Todd. By the way, how's your foot holding out?"

"Could be worse."

Howie stood up and hoisted his pack onto his shoulders. "About that great-uncle, Jess, you could tell him I need a new interior pack frame before this one falls apart."

"Will do. And if I remember rightly, your birthday is coming up in a few weeks, Howie."

"Yeah, and one thing my old man won't be giving me is a new pack. Last year he gave me four pairs of stretchable socks that deformed my big toes."

Todd let them pull ahead, using the quiet moment to recheck his altimeter against the contour lines on the map.

"Remember, stay on the shelf. The terrain all around is steep and broken."

"Roger," came the reply, already muffled by the

dense tangle of yellow cedar.

As the shelf became narrower and more steeply sloping, Todd's boots nosed the snow in search of secure footing. The kicking motion hurt his ankle and jolted a nerve ending which shot pain up his leg. A year ago he wouldn't have given this slope a passing thought. But now the snow particles sloughing loose underfoot and swishing over the shelf edge brought the sweat to his forehead. He should have taken out his ice axe earlier. Although balance was dicey, Todd managed to swing one arm around and pull it from his pack. Now with each step he could plunge his ice axe into the snow. The lines of the poem they'd been reading at school spun through his head like the softly swishing snow. "And that was the first I knew that a goat could slip, that a goat could slip ..."

Todd forced his eyes away from the cliffs to the bush ahead where Jess and Howie had disappeared. Couldn't they have waited for him? They knew he'd been checking the altimeter.

As he was chewing on these thoughts, a roar broke out overhead. "Helicopter!" No mistaking that sound in the mountains. It was a sound Todd disliked, one that always caught him off guard. A geologist, maybe? Too early in the season. Heliskiers? Not likely. They stuck to the more popular Whistler-Blackcomb area. Another party of climbers, then? Forget it. What would be the point of taking a helicopter into a reasonably accessible area? He swept the disquieting thoughts from his mind and hurried after the others.

Jess and Howie were waiting for him where the slope eased off.

"You look wiped," Jess said.

As if he needed to be told. "I should have stopped and taken off a sweater," he excused himself. "Did you see where that helicopter went?"

"We heard it, all right," Howie said, unzipping Todd's pack and pulling out the trail mix. "I figure it was carrying supplies into a logging camp somewhere — probably loaded with spuds and steaks and salad and apple pies with whipped cream. Those loggers know their grub. And speaking of food, I'm starved."

A logging camp or possibly a mining camp. Howie had stumbled on to the logical answer.

"Chocolate?" Howie pressed a square into his hand.

Todd forced it down. They still had a way to go and he needed the energy.

After an hour's steady slogging, they emerged from bush into alpine terrain. The high country lay deep under snow and would remain so until late summer when there would be a brief flash of flowers before winter's return. Todd's gaze swept the expanse of snow. No sign of other climbers. For the moment the Witch's Fang lay hidden from view somewhere beyond the next rise.

Jess handed him half a tuna sandwich.

"I'm not hungry for tuna," he told her.

"You should eat something, Todd."

"We shouldn't stop for long."

"Why not?" Howie said. "It's one-thirty and I'm ravenous. If you can't eat your sandwich, hand it over here."

After lunch they pushed on, swearing silently whenever the sun-softened snow sank underfoot. Gradually they stripped off extra sweaters and pile jackets until they were down to shirt sleeves. Todd smeared more sunscreen over his face and fitted the protective side flaps onto his dark glasses. He ought to have done it earlier. If eyes were left without proper protection at this altitude and at this time of year, the glare from the snow could cause snow blindness. He'd had a touch of it once after losing his dark glasses, and he had no wish to repeat the painful experience.

Todd was ahead of the others when the Witch's Fang first broke into view. Crouched in the snow, lava block balanced upon lava block, it seemed to be keeping pace with them as they moved higher. He could almost swear it was rising, thrusting itself upward like some living creature. And there was something else there too, something he didn't want to see — a tent sitting beneath the steep snowy flanks of the Witch's Fang. Situated on the last bit of level ground before the upward swirl of rock and snow, it looked out of place.

Howie caught up to Todd and grabbed his arm. "So that explains the helicopter. What was their big hurry, I wonder? And why put the tent there? I'd estimate the snow slope directly above it is thirty-five degrees, maybe more. With the sun working on the new snow higher up, the whole thing could avalanche. Wipe out the tent and everything."

Todd pulled the binoculars from his pack, focusing first on the campsite, then sweeping up the steep snow slope to where it ended in cliffs. Tracks directly below the rock! His hands were shaking as he handed the binocs to Howie.

"Take a look."

"Yeah, two figures immediately below the rock. Looking at the route, I imagine. Doing a recce before the big climb."

"Do you think it's Kurt?" Jess asked. "Let me look."

Todd grabbed his binoculars back. "How would I know? All I see is two black dots."

"Whoever they are, I wouldn't want to be on those steep snow slopes right now," Howie said. "I suggest we dump our packs, look for a campsite here and wander up later for a friendly chat."

They sat on their packs and watched as the shadow of the Witch's Fang gradually enveloped the small tent sitting below the snow slope, then slipped towards them. Although they were still in dazzling sunlight, there was a chill to the air. And soon their sun would be overtaken by the dark outline of the Witch's Fang.

"That old Witch's Fang almost seems alive," Jess whispered.

✧ CHAPTER 5

AFTER SCOUTING AROUND, they found a reasonably flat campsite beside a patch of stunted alpine fir. It was too early for streams to be open, but the snow had melted out around the bush-sized trees, leaving a depression filled with icy meltwater. Everywhere there was the sound of water: dripping from the bare rocks nearby, moving under the snow, drifting up from distant torrents and waterfalls in the valley. Snow everywhere, but summer was just around the corner.

Jess and Howie were pitching the tent and Todd was brewing some coffee when they heard the first warning sound. Like the drumming of a distant thunderstorm, the rumble of the avalanche grew and exploded down the snow slope above them. Todd upset the pan of water and Jess dropped her ice axe.

Finally the chaos of swirling snow gave way to silence — the long silence when time stands still.

As the toe of the avalanche slumped to a halt, Todd could almost feel its icy breath. He struggled to move, to say something. Howie was the first back to life.

"My god!" he whispered. "The avalanche swept those two people away. I saw them a second ago. And now they're gone."

Jess grabbed his arm. "No, I can still see a person moving up there."

Howie shaded his eyes. "You're right. I do see someone. Grab the empty pack from the tent, Jess. Throw in anything useful you can find — sleeping bag, extra sweater, first-aid kit, flashlights, whatever."

Todd's hands were shaking as he turned off the camp stove. By contrast, Jess and Howie appeared cool and organized.

Howie dived under the tent flap. "I can find only one shovel," he shouted.

"Mine's here," Todd said. "I was using it to level out the snow. Have you got yours, Jess?"

"I must have left it behind."

"Forgot your shovel! I reminded you twice. You told me you had it."

"I did have my shovel out, but in the last-minute rush I forgot it."

"Never mind," Howie said. "Two shovels are adequate, as long as we have our ice axes. Bring the stove, Todd."

Already Howie and Jess were shouldering their packs, preparing to move off.

"Sure, I'll bring it." He'd burned his thumb trying to close the darn thing. Along with the stove he dropped some dried soup packets, cheese and rye crisp into his pack. That should do. Wait a minute — his ice axe. He had forgotten the most important item. Jess and Howie were way ahead now.

Dream walking, shuffling a moon walk — everything felt unreal. This wasn't happening, and the car accident had never happened. He was a bystander, only a kid, damn it. These things happened to other people, not him. But the pain jabbing his left foot whenever he broke through the snow was the same pain he'd woken up to after the operation. Thank god for morphine and Demerol and whatever else they had given him.

Reality returned with his parents' arrival. I wonder if they are disgusted with me? Please, guys, don't cry. I'm going to be all right. Really.

Later, waiting on the tarmac for the air ambulance to Vancouver, he could feel the sky cooling and darkening after the long midsummer day. He was left alone for a moment, strapped to a stretcher. Under the pinpricks of stars he felt remote, cut off from everything and everybody. In a panic, he'd recited his personal creed over and over: "I'm Todd Rushton. I live in Vancouver. And I'm waiting for the air ambulance." Over and over. He couldn't forget anything, because if he did it might not come back — ever. Two-thirty a.m. Night flight from Prince George to Vancouver. Morning hung in the northeast, but south where he was heading it was dark. His body hurt with every move. And he felt so tired ...

"Are you coming, Todd? We've got to move." Jess's and Howie's voices nagged him from the distance.

Todd tried to focus on the scene ahead. A figure was moving around, crisscrossing the avalanche track. Against the backdrop of jumbled snow blocks and cliffs, the action looked futile.

"We have zero time to waste," he heard Howie warning. "If we don't recover whoever is buried there within the next thirty minutes or so, his chances of survival are slim."

As Todd moved closer, the small wiry figure bent over the snow straightened up and shook aside the dark hair covering his forehead.

"Kurt," Todd murmured.

"Surprise, eh? I'm sure you weren't expecting me."

"Not exactly." Todd could have sworn he saw a smile waver across Kurt's thin face.

"Who's buried?" Howie demanded. "Were you wearing avalanche transceivers?"

"Whoa down, one question at a time. Nice to see you two guys. I see you brought Jess along."

"Skip the formalities," Todd said. "There's somebody under the snow, right?"

"Leo. He's been there fifteen minutes."

Todd had met Leo a few times. Not a bad guy, he remembered. Younger than Kurt, though, and completely under his sway.

"You haven't answered Howie's question," Jess insisted. "Were you wearing Pieps?"

Kurt shook his head. "It was only a short recce before tomorrow's climb. Why bother?"

"You should have been wearing them. There was new snow followed by high temperatures — possible avalanche conditions."

"So? I've had way more experience in the mountains than you. Climbing is a calculated risk, like everything else."

"Too bad about Leo ..." Howie muttered. "Obviously there's no use turning our Pieps to receive."

Todd felt inside his sweater for the small instrument dangling from his neck. "You think there's any danger of a second avalanche?"

Howie shrugged. "I don't know how much snow is still hanging up there. We're wasting time."

"You're right, Howie." Todd unzipped the cover of his Pieps and moved the switch to transmit. Now if he was buried in snow, that little box would continue to broadcast its steady peep-peep from the frozen depths, reaching out a lifeline to the surface where another signal would be zeroing in. Todd patted his chest where this second heart was beating.

"How far ahead of you was Leo when the avalanche hit?" Howie asked.

"Forty metres, maybe. It caught him smack in the middle of the slope."

"Are there any bushes or rock outcrops where he could be hung up?"

"I doubt it."

"All right, we'll start the search right here — at the toe of the avalanche. Jess, stay low; Kurt, you go higher up and Todd and I will take the centre lines."

At Howie's signal they moved across the avalanche path in a row, probing the snow with their ice axes at regular intervals.

"I wish we had our ski poles along," Jess said as they were preparing to turn and start a fresh traverse. "We could unscrew them and turn them into half-decent avalanche probes."

"Yeah," Howie agreed. "I finally broke down and bought myself a pair of extendable poles. I swear by them."

"You can have all the climbing hardware and junk you want," Kurt said. "But what it boils down to in the end is luck."

"And for people like Leo, who go with you, mostly bad luck," Jess said.

"That's your opinion. What do you know about real climbing?"

Howie scuffed some snow at Jess. "Better cool it," he whispered.

"Mostly bad luck," Todd repeated the words. And because of Kurt they were involved in a mad scramble against time. What did he fear more? The emptiness of that probe into the frozen depths, or the sensation when his ice axe hit something solid — a chunk of ice, say, or a rock. After a while it was no longer Leo, the climber from their club, he was seeking, but rather some nameless, deformed object from the depths.

Howie clapped him on the back. "You're really jabbing your ice axe into the snow, man. Take it easy or you'll wear yourself out."

"How long have we been going, Howie?"

"Ten minutes."

"He's been buried over half an hour," Kurt said. "There's zero chance he's alive."

"Will you shut up," Todd snapped. "We take for granted Leo is still alive — period."

"Sure, if Leo had his jacket on and the hood was up, his chances are better ..." Howie started to say.

"I haven't a clue what he was wearing. He was way ahead of me."

Todd paused to stick another piece of red flagging into the snow, marking their course. It was getting cold in the shadows where they were. The sun had just left their campsite too. As he watched, the shadow cast by the Witch's Fang seemed to sweep across the expanse of alpine meadows, shifting the snow into deeper shades of blues and purples. Afternoon was moving on.

Todd shivered slightly and zipped up his jacket. From inside he could hear the rhythmic pulses coming from his avalanche transceiver. All movement was automatic now — probe down, probe up, step forward. Keep level with Jess and Howie. Probe down, probe up, step forward. Not too fast. He had practised this many times with his father and the mountain rescue team, but always practice, never for real. Step, probe. Step, probe … if nothing was found, they would keep repeating the operation until the whole slope had been covered. They weren't giving up, and Kurt was coming along, even if they had to drag him.

SPEED IS VITAL. Todd could almost see the black capital letters of the *Avalanche Manual* flashing at him from the snow. Half of all avalanche victims die within the first half hour. After that time, survival rates plummet rapidly.

Todd tried to blot out the bleak words. Probe down, probe up, step forward. Keep moving. They had covered the most likely area at the tongue of the avalanche and hadn't found anything. Perhaps he was buried too deeply. Why hadn't Kurt taken the proper precautions? You couldn't blame the mountain or fate for sheer human stupidity.

When Kurt stopped to put on his wool hat and gloves, the others pushed ahead. "I need a breather," he told them. "You go on and I'll catch up."

"If there's one person I detest, it's him," Jess said quietly.

"I agree one hundred percent."

"There's no point letting it show," Howie warned. "We're together here and we need Kurt's help."

As usual Howie was right. After a while Todd's thoughts wandered back to the *Avalanche Manual*.

In a wet snow avalanche, like the present one, the snow generally consolidates within minutes of stopping. If the victim manages to clear an airspace around his face, well and good. However, that space soon ices over with the moisture generated from breathing and rapidly becomes impervious.

A self-made tomb. Todd shuddered at his own words and tried to concentrate his energy on the next probe.

What would it sound like beneath that weight of snow? Hey buddy, down there, can you hear our voices and footsteps overhead? Sound is transmitted into snow reasonably well, but not out, the *Avalanche Manual* states. No point screaming for help then, unless you're within a few centimetres of the surface. It simply wastes the available air. But how to deal with the panic, alone in the darkness? Avalanche victims, in their confusion and fear, have been known to dig down, rather than up.

Todd glanced at his watch again. Another five minutes had gone by.

An icy cocoon. The image formed in his mind. Hypothermia would be gnawing away at the tiny, icy bundle, and if they didn't find it soon, the result would be certain death.

Todd knew only too well the various stages of hypothermia, mild through severe. Eventually the core body temperature drops below thirty degrees Celsius and the heart stops. Last spring he had been with Sam and the mountain rescue team when they'd located a hiker lost near Vancouver. He'd appeared dazed and incoherent and spilled the hot drink they'd offered him. Moderate hypothermia, their group leader had said. Already his muscles were stiffening and his pulse was erratic. Soon he would be too cold to shiver — almost a contradiction in terms, Todd thought.

An icy cocoon. The image kept returning.

Todd glanced along the probe line. Trust Kurt to have been lagging behind again. Beside him, but forging ahead now and again as if he couldn't hold himself back, was Howie — his shoulders hunched, his forehead furrowed, completely absorbed by the task. And Jess, how was she? Wait a minute! She was bent over the snow, pulling at something.

"A glove!" Jess shouted. "I've found a glove."

They tore at the snow with their shovels, ice axes, bare hands — whatever worked best.

"I've got Leo's arm," Howie said. "Can you feel any pulse, Jess?"

"My hands are so cold I can barely feel. Yes, I do have it. I have a pulse."

Todd felt the muscles at the back of his neck and shoulders relaxing. "Dig!" he shouted, drowning out his own crazy laughter. "Keep digging."

And the flying snow melted when it touched their burning faces until they had to lick away the drops with their tongues. They were like children frolicking in the snow, only this game was deadly serious.

DIG! Todd screamed silently at the Witch's Fang. Gouge with your old tooth, or give us a taste of fire and lava to melt this snow.

Jess leaned over Leo and very gently wiped the snow from his face. His eyelids flickered, but he didn't speak.

"I can feel some breath on my hand. His airways seem clear," she said. "I just wish I had more than basic first aid."

"I've got my industrial ticket, plus wilderness first aid," Kurt told her. "With two certificates I can get a job anywhere."

Good for you, Todd thought. As long as you're not working on me.

"You should take over, then," Jess said.

"Carry on. You're not doing badly, considering. I'm here if you need my expertise."

"Oh, thanks a lot," Jess said under her breath. "You better be ready in case an emergency comes up and we have to do artificial respiration or something."

"Don't worry, I'll stick around."

"Be careful moving him," she warned as Todd and Howie slipped a foamie and sleeping bag under Leo. "We don't know what injuries he has."

Todd watched his sister as she bent over Leo. Standard first aid, that's all Jess had, plus a few workshops in cardiopulmonary rescuscitation. They had taken the course together last fall, but alongside his clumsy performance she looked like a real pro.

He could hear Jess talking quietly, reminding herself of all the necessary steps. "Insulation under the body, a quick examination — no serious bleeding or obviously broken bones."

For the first time Todd noticed a slight shaking of her hands. Howie must have seen it too, because kneeling down, he gave her a quick hug. "You're doing great, Jess. Keep it up. We're all ready to help."

Leo's eyelids flickered open, then shut again. Had he recognized them? Todd wondered. And that face — Todd couldn't get over the colour, or rather the lack of it. Against the snow Leo's face appeared almost transparent, as if one could trace the leaflike pattern of veins through his skin. His eyelids opened again.

"Leo, can you hear me?" Jess asked.

His lips moved, but no sound came.

"Let me try," Kurt said.

"Go ahead."

"Leo, it's me — Kurt. Do you remember what happened?"

"You don't need to yell," Jess told him. "Go closer. Ask him if he can move his legs, if he feels any pain."

"Can you move your legs?"

A tremor shook Leo, as if he was still struggling against the weight of snow.

"Well, does anything hurt?"

His lips moved. "Cold."

"I'm worried about moving him down to the

tent," Jess said, "but we have to start warming him right away."

"How about we each take a corner of the sleeping bag," Howie suggested, "and hold it tight like a stretcher."

"It's probably the best way." Jess stood up and took a deep breath.

Howie rolled up one corner inside his fist and motioned Kurt to take the other side. "I think Kurt and I can manage here, if you two take the back corners."

"It's a long way down to the tent," Kurt complained, "and we're walking over avalanche crud the whole way."

"You don't have to remind us," Jess said. "You're lucky the tent wasn't swept away by the avalanche. It's a dumb place to camp."

"Not at all, Jessica. The tent was placed there deliberately, as close to the Witch's Fang as possible. If you notice, the tent is sitting on a slight rise in order to deflect any snow."

"There are plenty of flat places lower down where we are," Todd pointed out. "Why risk going that close to a steep slope?"

"Why? Speed, of course. Climb the Witch's Fang, then get out."

"And hire a helicopter on the long weekend because you heard rumours of other climbing parties."

"Could be." Kurt smiled. "I guess you heard our helicopter overhead."

"Unfortunately, yes."

Todd stumbled and almost fell. The sudden movement jerked the sleeping bag.

"Watch it," Howie cautioned. "These avalanche blocks are wickedly slippery. If we go without talking, I guarantee Leo will have a smoother ride."

"Always the reasonable man, aren't you, Howie?"

"Sometimes, Kurt. It depends how far I'm pushed."

Todd glanced over at his sister. Her neck muscles were straining with the heavy load. "We're almost there, Jess. Just a few more steps."

"I can't hold on much longer. My arm muscles are giving out."

"Let me help," Todd offered. "Being the shortest, you get more of the weight."

"Women are whiners," Kurt said. "That's why I hate going on trips with them. They never do their fair share."

"That's not true, Kurt. My sister has been doing most of the work."

Jess gritted her teeth. "Thanks, Todd. I can manage the last few steps."

Howie stopped beside the tent. "Okay, Kurt, open the tent flaps. Hold the sleeping bag taut and we'll try and ease him through."

Before slipping into the tent, Jess turned to Todd. "I'm worried about Leo. I hope I can manage."

He watched as she tilted her head towards the Witch's Fang that loomed dark against the evening sky.

"Let's not go there tomorrow."

"You're tired and cold, Jess. You'll feel better after a bite to eat. Look, I'll stay out here and cook up some soup."

"That would be nice."

A breath of wind stirred somewhere high on the Witch's Fang. It dropped over the cliffs, slid down the snow slope and jostled the loose particles of snow at Todd's feet. And then it was gone. Alone now, Todd listened to the voices rising and falling inside the tent.

"Better take his boots off."

"Lucky he had his anorak on and a pile jacket underneath."

"That probably saved him."

"Are you going into the sleeping bag with him, Kurt?"

"I suppose so. My god, he feels like a block of ice. This won't work."

"It has to. There's no other way of warming him here. You better crank up your body heat, Kurt."

"Can you hear us, Leo?"

"Look at our blue baby nodding his head."

Laughter finally and more talk.

Standing alone in the cold, Todd felt his resentment growing. Not counting Leo, why were they all warm and cosy except him? Kurt should have been the one freezing his butt off, seeing he had wrecked their plans. Jess was dubious now about continuing the climb, and if he knew Howie, he'd probably side with her.

Todd packed more snow into the cooking pot, placed it over the camp stove, then crouched down to savour the spluttering and crackling of the water drops. The roar of the stove suited his mood perfectly.

Jess's voice came through clearly. "Don't try to talk, Leo. Just nod when I ask a question. Does the right leg hurt — here or higher up? Is it the knee?"

With each handful of snow that Todd threw into the pot, steam billowed up and the water level rose. Soon he'd be able to add the soup. Todd reached into his pack, pulled out two packets of instant onion soup, split them open with his Swiss army knife and spilled the contents into the boiling water. Later he'd add a touch of Parmesan cheese and *voilà*! Whew ... with that oniony-smelling steam tickling his nose, it was hard to stay angry.

Howie's head appeared through the tent flaps. "Do I smell soup, lovely onion soup?" He crouched down beside Todd. "You must be freezing."

"The warmth from the stove helps. How's Leo doing?"

"His right knee is bothering him. Jess thinks it's a ligament. His leg probably got twisted by the force of the snow."

"He's lucky to be alive. Have you given any thought to how we get him out?"

"Kurt says a helicopter is scheduled to pick

them up the day after tomorrow."

"So he not only hires a helicopter to beat every-one else here, but he's also too lazy to walk out." Todd stirred the soup furiously with the blade of his army knife.

"We're lucky a helicopter is coming," Howie reminded him.

"Granted. Can Leo hang on the extra day?"

"No prob. He doesn't have any pain unless he moves around, and Jess gave him a bunch of painkillers for the night."

"What did Kurt say about tomorrow?"

"He'll have to stay with Leo, of course."

"Did Kurt say that?"

"Not exactly."

"Because I wouldn't be too sure with Kurt."

"Talk to him yourself, then."

"I hate talking to the guy."

Todd gave the soup a final stir and sprinkled some Parmesan cheese on top. When he turned off the stove, the flame faded, the roar died to a hum and finally to silence.

"Soup's on," he announced, handing the pot to Howie.

Todd left his boots under the outer tent flap where the rest of the gear was stored and crawled inside. Cosy for sure! It was a three-person tent and they were five now. Coming from near dark-ness, he found that the sudden brightness made him blink. Everyone was wearing headlamps ex-cept for Leo, who was zipped up beside Kurt in two sleeping bags. Jess had placed her candle lantern near the soup pot, and everyone was tucking in. Hmm, he better get busy before Howie polished everything off.

"Man, is this soup excellent," Howie said, sucking shreds of onion from his spoon. "If anybody has leftovers, you know where to send them."

Holding his cup in both hands, Todd waited for the surge of blood into his hands and feet, the ache that would gradually give way to soothing warmth. He took off his socks. Boy, the place sure reeked: damp socks, smoke, onion soup. He glanced over at Kurt, who was leaning on one elbow, trying to drink his soup.

"What are your plans for tomorrow, Kurt?"

"I'll be hanging around camp and keeping an eye on Leo here. What about you?"

"I haven't the foggiest." Careful. Kurt was watching him with a look that breathed more of blue glacial depths than human warmth.

How was Leo faring beside Kurt? His eyes were closed. Probably asleep. And small wonder after the shock of the accident and now the sudden warmth radiating from another body. For surely there was warmth somewhere in Kurt, deep within the core.

"When the core body temperature drops below a certain point, another source of heat must be found immediately or the temperature will continue to fall." In spite of the warm bodies jammed inside the tent, the words from the *Avalanche*

Manual made him shiver.

Todd stuck his head through the entrance until he could see the outline of the Witch's Fang merging with the night sky. It was cold, all right. As he stared upward, a chunk of snow broke loose from somewhere and exploded down the cliffs. Strange that it should come loose now, long after the warmth of the day. A sudden gust of wind perhaps, a boulder shifting somewhere? Or ... Todd hesitated, could it be some movement in the earth's crust, a surge of lava within subterranean chambers? But all the old volcanoes, peaks like Mt. Garibaldi and the Black Tusk were extinct. Oh, yeah? What about Mt. St. Helens blowing its top and Mt. Baker spewing sulphur at a steady rate? Where was that dividing line between extinct and dormant?

"Dormant." Todd repeated the ominous-sounding word. Dormant like some ancient beast of prey biding its time — not human time — but the time of Ice Ages, coming and going, of continents emerging, of mountain ranges rising and folding.

✧ CHAPTER 6

TODD CLOSED THE OUTER TENT FLAP and retreated to the warmth inside. "It's late," he said. "We should be thinking about leaving."

"No prob," Howie told him. "We have our headlamps. Besides, I'm enjoying the food and the company."

"Especially mine," Leo said from the sleeping bag. "I'm the life of the party, you know."

Kurt pushed him under the sleeping bags.

"You better finish defrosting before you come up with another joke."

Kurt appreciating a joke? Todd shook his head. In the flickering candlelight, his expression appeared almost benign.

"Hey, Kurt," Howie was asking, "tell us a bit about your Yosemite trip. You did a few solo climbs, right?"

"I didn't do anything but solo climb. I went down there by myself."

"He wouldn't take me," Leo complained. "Said I wasn't up to scratch."

"Yosemite isn't for novice climbers, Leo."

"What's it like?" Howie insisted.

"Like no other place. Soloing is the way to go — the only way. No distractions, no ropes or climbing hardware to stand in the way. There's simply you and the grey rock and the sharpness of the wind and the blue sky. And the fear is there too, trying to slice through your concentration."

"The fear?" Howie asked. "I didn't think you ever felt afraid."

Don't keep egging him on, Todd thought. I don't want to listen.

Kurt shrugged. "I didn't say I was. But let fear get in the way only once, and you fall because you're afraid to fall. Crazy, eh?"

"Yeah, you have to be supremely confident of your abilities to go solo. Speaking for myself, I like company and the support that gives."

Kurt stared at Howie for a moment without saying anything.

Todd looked at his watch. It was after ten o'clock. Now was his chance to get a word in.

"Listen, Howie, our campsite is a disaster area. We should be going down."

"Planning an early start?" Kurt asked.

"I don't know any more what we're doing."

"You'll have to wait a minute," Jess said, "because I want to see Leo finish his soup."

"My soup has gone cold, and I've run out of

steam too," Leo said. "I can't finish this second cup, Jess."

"Pass it over to Howie, then."

"Thanks, Leo. I'll polish it off. If you and Kurt weren't out of commission," Howie went on, "I'd suggest we join forces and climb the Witch's Fang tomorrow."

Are you nuts, Howie? Even Jess was staring at him in amazement.

"It's out of the question," was all Kurt said. A minute later he rolled over and closed his eyes. No more talk, no thank-yous, no goodbyes.

"I feel like a Siamese twin," Leo apologized. "I can't stay awake either."

"No wonder," Jess said. "Sleep is exactly what you need after all you've been through. We'll look in on you tomorrow, Leo."

"Thanks. If it wasn't for you three, I wouldn't be sitting here. Next time I wear my Pieps."

"No prob." Howie cuffed him on the shoulder as they left.

Outside, Todd zipped up his jacket and flipped the hood over his head. "Chilly," he remarked.

No point talking. Jess and Howie had linked arms and were running and hop-skipping down the frozen slope, shouting like a couple of nursery-school kids. He'd better try to catch up. There was no need of headlamps. A moon rising over the mountain ranges to the east was flooding the landscape in a soft light and casting elongated shadows from every ridge and hummock. With their shadows galloping along behind, mimicking every twist and turn, they became a trio of fierce mountain giants.

Curses — he stumbled over the same cooking pot he'd upset earlier that afternoon. What a mess! A tent flap had worked itself loose and was flailing monotonously in the wind.

"Got you!" Howie wrestled the tent flap to the ground.

"Great, except now you're covered with snow. Bend over, and I'll brush you off."

"Thanks for swishing it down my neck, Jess."

"I can't speak for you two," Todd said, kicking the snow off his boots, "but my feet are freezing and I'm heading into the tent."

"Good idea. I'll pass in the gear," Howie said.

"Let me clear some space first. It's a mess in here."

A few minutes later they were all jammed inside the small mountain tent, except for Howie's legs, which were still hanging outside.

"Can't get my boots off," he complained. "The laces are frozen. Lend me your army knife, Todd."

"I want it back, Howie."

Howie dug at the laces with the pick. "You know there are high-altitude climbers who routinely sleep with their boots on to keep them from freezing up. Personally, I get my kicks elsewhere."

Groans from the other two. "Howie, you are not wearing boots tonight," Todd insisted.

"You know what?" Jess said. "We forgot our

sleeping bag up there."

"You forgot it, Jess. Why didn't you put it back in your pack?"

"Because it was damp from carrying Leo."

"Well, I'm not going way up there now to collect a sleeping bag."

"Quit it, you two," Howie interrupted. "I'll share a sleeping bag with Todd. And with your two classy down jackets, we sure aren't going to freeze."

"How be I make some hot chocolate to warm us up?" Jess said.

"Good idea." Todd reached outside, found the cooking pot that he had already filled with snow and set it on the stove by the tent entrance. Soon the familiar roar was drowning out everything else.

Howie kept his headlamp aimed at the steaming pot. "I'm ravenous. How about I make some instant soup?"

"Wait till I get our hot-chocolate water." Jess dipped three cups into the boiling water. "Now you can go for it, Howie."

Todd watched as he emptied a package of tomato soup into the remaining water. Afterwards he opened the instant potatoes and let the flakes pour into the cooking pot until Todd grabbed the bag away.

"You're crazy, Howie. It'll be straight concrete."

"I'm hungry," Howie insisted.

"You can't be that hungry — not after all the salami, rye bread and onion soup we had earlier."

"I'm always hungry. The old man and I are such lousy cooks I'm probably suffering from terminal malnutrition."

"I'll invite you to dinner again when we get home," Jess promised.

Howie placed the cooking pot in the middle of the tent where everyone could reach.

"To heck with climbing," he said. "It seems we spend half our time cooking, eating or talking about eating."

"I hope you don't mean that seriously, Howie. I came up here to climb the Witch's Fang."

"Just kidding."

"I'd like to get as early a start as possible."

"And you want to keep right on schedule in spite of the accident?" Jess asked.

"Why not? We know Leo is okay."

"We need to discuss this," Howie said. "But give me a few minutes — okay? My mashed potatoes are getting cold."

After a few spoonfuls of the sticky mess, Todd and Jess collapsed onto the sleeping bags. The stove and the warmth from their three bodies had taken the chill off the air. Todd closed his eyes and listened to Howie's spoon methodically scraping the bottom of the cooking pot.

Howie sighed and burped. "Excuse me, folks, but that was excellent."

No one spoke for a while, but Todd could sense Jess's reluctance growing.

"It's eleven-thirty," he said, shining the headlamp on his watch. "We should turn in now if we want an early start tomorrow."

Todd felt Howie sinking back onto the sleeping bag. Clever fellow — lying there like a lump in the darkness, not saying a word.

"I don't feel good about going," Jess said finally. "I suppose it's the accident."

"But Leo is fine. We saw him sitting up, drinking soup before we left."

"I know."

"Look — you're tired, Jess. You had the major responsibility of caring for Leo, and you did a great job. After a good night's sleep, I'm sure you'll feel different."

"Possibly."

Howie stirred and rolled over.

Here it comes, Todd thought. Neither of them was really committed to the climb, and the accident would provide the logical escape route. Howie would support Jess, and tomorrow would be totally wasted hanging around camp, their one chance blown.

"You know, Jess, I think we ought to go," Howie said finally. "Your brother has a lot of time and energy invested in this climb. Weather is good and we're perfectly situated here."

"Perfectly situated," Jess echoed. "And what about Leo?"

"We'll be going past their tent first thing in the morning. If Leo isn't fine, we call it quits then. Agreed?"

"All right," Jess said finally, "but I'll hold you to your promise."

Good old Howie. He should never have suspected the guy. "So I'll set my watch for five-thirty?"

"Six-thirty," Jess said.

"Six," Todd countered.

"And six it is," Howie declared. "Now good night, everybody. I'd love some sleep if you two would let me."

"'Night."

"Sleep well."

Finally. But try as he might, Todd couldn't sleep. His legs felt stiff and his foot ached after the unaccustomed exercise. If he started twisting and turning, it would wake the others. Howie was stretched out beside him, clutching their joint sleeping bag and snoring — or snuffling, as he preferred to call it. On his other side Jess was resting quietly. Lucky them.

Once or twice Todd felt his whole body jump — the alarming start that happens between sleeping and waking. Images of the Witch's Fang, of Kurt Stone, drifted through his mind. He was driving somewhere with Kurt. The road took them across high plateau country, mile after mile. There were no other cars. And always in the distance was some unknown mountain range. His head began to nod. Unexpectedly, the road veered into a narrow, twisting canyon. Todd yelled a warning and reached for the wheel, but Kurt refused to slow down. When

Todd saw the look in his eyes, he shrank back. The emptiness of the far horizon was there, where distance drains away all colour and only a cold shimmering is left.

Fire and Ice.

Todd woke at the sound of the words. Had he spoken them out loud and if so, why? Someone else was stirring. "Jess …?"

The tent entrance was partially open, and through the gap Todd could see the moon sliding behind the Witch's Fang. A wisp of cloud encircled the summit, like steam seething from some unknown source.

Jess stumbled into the tent, catching her head on the zippered flap.

"What's the trouble, Jess?"

"I hate having to go out in the middle of the night, especially with that mountain of yours hanging over me. I'd swear it was moving."

"Cloud effects, Jess. And don't call it my mountain."

"Well, you're the one who wants to climb it."

"Come on, Jess, we all want to." Howie caught her by the legs and pulled her down. "No changing your mind in the middle of the night."

"I thought you were asleep, Howie."

"With you two arguing?" He shone the headlamp on his watch. "Two o'clock. If everyone shuts up, we have exactly four more hours of sleep."

Howie rolled over, dragging the sleeping bag with him, and was soon snuffling peacefully.

Relax, Todd told himself, retrieving his share of the sleeping bag. Howie can't help snoring. His sinuses get plugged because he's allergic to down sleeping bags. So why doesn't he buy another bag instead of keeping everyone awake? Because he can't afford to, that's why. If he does have any extra cash, it goes straight into climbing equipment. Finally Todd stuffed some tissue in his ears and pulled his wool cap down to muffle the sound.

The moon was shining against the wall of the tent, creating a false sense of warmth. It had passed beyond the Witch's Fang and was sailing alone in the night sky. Feeling very much awake, Todd watched its slow descent towards the ridge. Now there would be a few hours of real darkness before the sun began to light the eastern horizon. Only when Todd had given up any idea of sleep did he finally drift off.

✧ CHAPTER 7

TODD PULLED HIS ARM from the sleeping bag and looked at his watch. Seven. They had slept through the alarm. Now they would be lucky to get away by eight.

In spite of sleepy protests, Todd shook the other two awake, then stumbled outside to start the stove. While waiting for it to lapse into a steady hum, he stared up at the other tent. No signs of life there yet.

"What's the weather doing?" Howie asked.

"It's perfect, except we should have been on our way two hours ago. Are you coming?"

"Soon as I smell coffee."

"I'll have some snow melting in a minute. You won't have an excuse then, Howie."

Overnight the snow had frozen into a solid crust. A few whacks with his ice axe and Todd broke through to more granular stuff underneath. He lumped handful after handful into the pot.

"Won't be long," he said.

"How cold is it out there?" Jess asked.

"Chilly, and it will be until we have sun. But that's no excuse to stay in your sleeping bag, Jess."

"Will you quit nagging me, Todd. I'm coming."

"Well, I don't appreciate having to wait around."

"No prob, we're coming, Todd." There was a shriek as Howie dragged off her sleeping bag.

Todd couldn't help smiling. He dropped more snow into the pot, listening to it sizzle against the metal sides. Steam rose up — not long and it would be boiling. If he could just get those two moving. Luckily Howie could never resist the smell of coffee, even the instant junk. Todd filled the three cups with steaming water and, after stirring in the coffee, let the aroma drift through the open tent flap. It worked. A few seconds later Howie lurched out.

"Mmm, coffee. Attaboy, Todd." He cradled the warm cup in his hand.

Todd checked his watch again — half-past seven. They were way behind schedule, but at least they were making some progress. And then the familiar, stomach-churning apprehension struck. Sooner or later most climbers feel it, often not sleeping well or anticipating all the things that can go wrong. From past experience Todd knew his worst time was at breakfast, when his body still felt hung-over from sleep. First came the lack of appetite, then a sense of unreality or nagging anxiety.

"More coffee, Todd?"

"No thanks."

"Some bread then?"

"I've had enough, Howie."

"You've hardly eaten a thing."

"I'm not hungry. Maybe later."

"Take mine," Jess said, offering him some bread with jam and cheese. "I can't finish it."

"Look, I really don't want anything. I had some granola."

"I'll take it," Howie said. "No wonder you two are so skinny."

"It's Jess who doesn't eat. I usually have a huge breakfast, Howie, only this morning I'm not hungry."

Talking was an effort. Todd stomped his feet, trying to keep warm. And looking up at their route, still shrouded in cold shadows, didn't ease the anxiety. This was no afternoon stroll. Some sun would certainly help. Already it was hitting the peak, and soon it would be rolling down the steep rocky flanks onto the snow slopes and then bursting against Kurt and Leo's tent. That should wake them!

"Are we almost ready?" Todd asked. Once they were moving he'd feel better.

"Wait a sec," Jess said. "We don't want to waste the leftover coffee water."

Todd held out his plastic bottle. "You can pour the rest in here."

Howie was doing a last-minute rundown of

climbing gear. "We have two climbing ropes — one regular, the other lightweight. Everyone should have a few chocks, some slings, maybe three or four carabiners. Ice axes are a given. Bring your crampons. If we don't, we'll need them for sure. And what about an ice screw or two, in case we hit a gnarly section?"

"It seems like more to carry," Todd said. "But suit yourself."

"Okay, I'll leave them. But I will pack a couple of pitons and my piton hammer."

"Stop right there," Jess said. "You can never leave anything behind. Our packs are bursting. I won't take another thing."

Howie grinned foolishly. "Yeah, I know, Jess. And the rock is so rotten we'll probably never use my hardware."

Todd checked his watch again. "It's after eight, you two."

"No prob," Howie said. "I'm packing the stove. You start on."

"Howie, we don't need the stove. We aren't planning to bivouac on the Witch's Fang," Jess protested.

"Just in case."

Todd adjusted the hip belt on his pack and slung the heavier climbing rope around his shoulders. "I'm starting on. You two can catch up."

With each step his shoulders relaxed, and the cold and the tension seemed to flow out through his boot soles. Howie and Jess caught up to him near the other tent, where they broke through the shadow barrier into dazzling sunlight.

"There's no sign of life," Todd whispered. "Shall we wake them up or carry on?"

"We have to wake them," Jess insisted. "Don't you remember our bargain? We continue the climb only if we're sure Leo is okay."

"I hadn't forgotten, Jess. Don't jump to conclusions."

Howie lifted a pot from the camp stove that was sitting outside the tent. "The water isn't frozen. Somebody was up early this morning."

"Kurt was," came a sleepy voice from the tent. "He left around six o'clock this morning. I told him not to go alone. I practically got down on my hands and knees and begged him to wait for you guys. I must have argued for half an hour — the whole time he was making breakfast — before he told me to shut up. I don't think he heard a word I said."

"Left for where?" Todd demanded.

"The Fang — where else?"

"Wild man." Howie whistled. "I wonder if he was figuring on this all along?"

"Don't ask me. I must have been dead asleep when he crawled out. There was no alarm or anything. It's amazing how he managed to wake that early."

"Not if you know Kurt," Todd muttered. "Did he say anything about his route?"

"Only that he didn't like yesterday's recce, that he intended to go look at the north ridge."

"Which means he won't be dropping loose rock overhead — one bonus, I suppose."

"For sure not on my head," Jess said, "because I'm staying here with Leo."

"Look, don't change any plans because of me. Other than feeling a bit stiff and tired, I'm fine. I won't starve either. There are a couple of sandwiches left over from yesterday, plus a bottle of orange juice. If you don't go, I'll feel guilty."

"How's the knee?" Howie asked.

"I can move around some."

"You don't mind being alone?"

"Mind? I plan to sleep all day, until Kurt gets back. From what we saw yesterday, I doubt he'll be staying long. The whole mountain is crumbling."

You don't know Kurt, Todd thought.

"What do you say, Jess? Leo thinks he can survive on his own. Should we keep your brother happy and go on?"

Todd watched as she studied the route ahead of them; the steep snow slope, narrowing into what looked like an even steeper gully, bounded by cliffs on each side. And above that the ridge sweeping towards the summit, invisible from where they were standing.

"I said I'd go if Leo feels all right. I hope I won't regret my promise."

"Are you positive, Jess?" Howie asked. "You don't sound totally enthusiastic."

"I'll be okay, Howie. The accident put a damper on my enthusiasm, that's all."

"As I said before, I think it would be neat to climb the Witch's Fang — the fact it's unclimbed is icing on the cake, but being with you guys is the main thing. I don't mind changing our plans if anyone feels happier."

Todd groaned. Did Howie always have to be such a saint? "I thought we had decided. We're wasting our time here talking."

"Okay, if that's how everyone feels." Howie turned to Leo. "Can we help you before we head on. Get the stove going? Make coffee? Start some porridge?"

"Thanks, but I'm hitting the sack again. I'll eat later. You people should be travelling if you want to make it back in daylight."

Todd shouldered his pack. "Leo's right. We should be going."

As they moved away, Leo called from the tent. "The gully looks exceedingly messy. Getting onto the rock face above the snow will be the crux."

"Thanks," Todd called back.

Leo grinned apologetically. "I guess the only thing you can thank me for is yesterday's avalanche. It should ease your minds knowing that snow isn't hanging over your heads. See you later."

A short distance beyond the tent, they came to yesterday's avalanche track. Overnight the debris had frozen solid and now, in the early-morning sunlight, the upturned chunks reflected a clear ice blue. Leo was one lucky man to have escaped alive, Todd thought. And Kurt? It was amazing he had the stomach to head off alone after yesterday's near tragedy.

"I've studied the air photos and maps of the Witch's Fang," Todd said. "Kurt doesn't have a hope on the north ridge. So why go?"

Howie shrugged. "You've done your homework. Maybe Kurt hasn't."

"I doubt this was a spur-of-the-moment decision."

"Your guess is as good as mine, Todd. Last night when we were together, I thought I was beginning to understand Kurt, to connect somehow. I mean, we all love climbing, right? Maybe we were being too judgemental. But now the guy up and leaves Leo and goes off by himself without talking to us."

"Nobody knows Kurt," Jess pointed out, "least of all you, Howie. I can't imagine two people more different. His going off alone this morning is typical. Because we're trying the south ridge, he has to try the north ridge."

"You're probably right, Jess." At least Todd hoped it was Kurt's contrariness taking him to the north ridge and not something he'd discovered yesterday during their recce.

Where the snow slope began to steepen, they stopped to take off their heavy sweaters and put on sunglasses. Todd checked his watch. Almost eight-thirty. Kurt would be well on his way if he'd left camp at six. In contrast they were standing at the bottom of a steep snow slope that ended in a sheer rock wall below the ridge — nowhere, to be exact.

Was the rock even climbable? Difficult to say. But one thing was certain — with each passing moment the sun was growing warmer and working on the terrain above them. The rubble of the gully was bonded together by frost, ice and snow, which was one reason for coming early in the season. They were definitely on the late side. Over the years Sam had repeated his little sermon *ad nauseam.* "If you want to climb the Witch's Fang, go early. Don't give her time to shed her frosty covering, because you might not like what's underneath."

Sometimes his father's flowery language annoyed him. It sounded so old-fashioned. And once revved up, he was oblivious to everyone and everything.

"How come you're just standing there?" Jess asked him. "We're putting on crampons."

"Crampons?"

"Yeah," Howie said. "It'll be faster with crampons and safer too. The snow is still rock-hard down here. If it gets soft higher up, we'll have them off in a minute."

Todd pulled the metal spikes from his pack and placed them side by side on the snow. He hadn't tried them out before coming — a definite mistake. No problem with the right foot, but as soon as he stepped onto the left crampon he felt insecure, and the sensation worsened as he tightened the straps linking his boots to the thin metal spikes. This was it — there was no turning back now.

"Hard candy, Todd?" Howie was peering into his face and offering him a fruit drop.

"Thanks, Howie." He brushed off the lint and stray hairs before popping it in his mouth. Probably been bouncing around in his pack since last summer. Never mind, Howie meant well.

"Are your Pieps turned on?" Howie asked.

Todd reached inside the light vest he was wearing and switched his avalanche transceiver on. He hoped Jess hadn't noticed. At least he had his climbing helmet on, which is more than Jess could claim.

"Where's your helmet?" he asked.

"In my pack."

"How come you're not wearing it?"

"I was leaving it until the last moment. You know I hate helmets. They make my head hot and itchy and they look stupid."

"Wearing a helmet is like doing up your seat belt in a car," Todd said, knowing this would make her furious.

Howie scrunched the helmet down on her head. "You look great."

"What a liar!"

"Are we ready?" Todd asked.

"As soon as I do up my helmet."

Todd took a few tentative steps. Placing the crampon points at a right angle to the slope demanded impossible flexibility from a foot that had been badly crushed. Within five minutes his ankle was hurting.

Howie drew up beside him. "Is the foot hurting?"

"A bit."

"Give me the rope, anything heavy you're carrying. If the going gets too rough, take your crampons off and I'll cut steps."

"I can manage."

Jess gave him a friendly tap. "Don't worry about us. Set your own pace."

Set my own pace? Oh, sure, he thought. If I could, I'd be flying up to intercept Kurt before he discovers the key to the north ridge — a hidden chimney maybe, a dihedral of firm rock, a crack where a chock could be inserted for a foolproof belay ...

Todd was moving diagonally up the snow slope, which he estimated to be between thirty-five and forty degrees. Much steeper and he'd have to face into the slope, using the front points on his crampons. No need for such extreme measures yet. Still, thirty-five degrees or so and a hard surface demanded respect, apart from the fact he was moving clumsily. The problem was maintaining balance with a foot that wouldn't respond to the flow of the slope.

Todd shifted the ice axe to his upper hand, ready to dig the pick-end in should he unexpectedly slip. On paper, self-arrest sounded so simple: you fell, rolled over on your stomach and with your whole body weight pressing down on the axe you eventually came to a stop. All very neat and tidy.

In real life falls tended to be messier, he thought. Like car accidents. A heavy pack could shift and drag you down headfirst. And what about the difficulty of rolling over on a steep surface before you gained incredible speed and smashed into rocks below? Ice axes, if they weren't wrenched from your hand by the fall, had a nasty habit of inflicting damage on vulnerable parts of the body. Crampons could be even more deadly. And, face it, falls by definition never come in handy locations.

Whew! After half an hour's hard slogging, Todd stopped to check Sam's altimeter.

"We're close to fifteen hundred metres," he announced, "which leaves approximately six hundred metres to the ridge, plus another three hundred or so to the top."

It didn't sound like much, but a world of ice, snow and crumbling rock lay between them and the summit.

"Distance-wise, a mere hike," Howie said. "Who knows, maybe we'll make it back in time for tea. Got any chocolate-chip cookies left, Jess?"

"Put food out of your mind, Howie."

Delicately poised for the next turn, with his ice axe serving as a third point of balance, Todd was only too aware of their altitude gain. Far below them the two tents were splotches of colour in an otherwise white world. Move the focus down and you came to the rim of trees breaking against the snow, wave after wave of alpine fir struggling to gain a foothold. The valley, the logging roads and the highway were beyond the horizon of thought, another world away.

Time to swivel around and kick the crampons into the snow. His left leg was trembling from the strain. Rest for an instant, leaning into the snow. Forward again, this time diagonally left. Swing the leg, punch the crampons in — swing and punch, swing and punch. I'd feel more secure with the rope, Todd thought. No rocks or crevasses below, but it was a mighty long way to slide, and avalanche debris doesn't make a soft landing. With thoughts like these, he'd never make it as a climber.

"Want me to take over the lead?" Howie asked. "I could hack out the occasional step."

"We don't have time to cut steps, Howie. I'll keep going."

The slope was steepening ahead. And the pain in his foot was increasing too. Perhaps he should let someone else take over. Did he imagine they could stop every few moments because of a smattering of pain? Poor kid, can't do it on his own ...

"You're not trying hard enough, Todd," the physiotherapist's voice cut in. "You have to start the exercises right away and then stick with them."

What did they expect from him? Fresh from an operation — metal pins in his femur and ankle, a tube stuck into his hand, Demerol or morphine every few hours to dull the pain ...

"Todd, I want you to sit up on the side of the bed.

Now, holding onto my arm, put some weight on your legs."

"I can't."

"I'm sure you can," the physiotherapist said. "Let's show your mother what you can do."

"They let me come early, Todd, before regular visiting hours."

He avoided his mother's eyes, looking instead at her hands. Her fingers curled and uncurled, wanting to stretch out, support his weight, stop the pain.

"Very good, Todd. Now take a step."

I won't cry out again. I won't ...

"Hey, Todd, have a breather and I'll take over. No, don't argue this time." Howie was beside him.

"I don't know how you keep up the pace," Jess said. "I'm wiped."

"I didn't realize I was going fast."

"Twice I asked you to slow down."

"Sorry, I never heard."

Todd let his friend move ahead. For a while the only sounds were the crunch of crampons against snow and the scrape from Howie's ice axe as he gouged out the occasional foothold. No point kidding myself, Todd thought. Howie's doing it for me. Otherwise he would never be cutting steps here. Look at him go — swing the ice axe, glide forward — one fluid motion. It was impressive to watch.

"How are you doing?" Jess asked.

"I'm feeling it in my legs."

"Me too. In spite of what Howie thinks, I'm out of shape for everything except ballet."

As the slope steepened, Howie left the diagonal and began moving straight up. Each time he placed a crampon a shower of ice crystals cascaded over their heads.

"My luck to be first." He grinned down at them like some mischievous mountain imp.

The steeper slope also increased the stress on Todd's ankle. For a moment he paused on one of Howie's laboriously hacked out platforms to rub the back of his leg. The left calf was shaking from the unaccustomed strain. Good thing he hadn't dropped physio over the winter as he'd been tempted to do.

"Another thirty metres or so and I'll be at the rock face," Howie called down.

Where our real troubles begin, Todd thought. He made the mistake of glancing over his shoulder to see where Jess was. Nothing but empty space there. What was keeping her? The sudden steepness, followed by a slight easing of the angle, had blotted out all traces of their campsite below. They were alone now, cut off from the valley with its pungent smells of alpine fir, black coffee brewing over the stove, onion soup, sweaty socks ...

Jess's head appeared over the rise, gradually filling the empty space.

"Hi, Jess."

"Hi."

"How's it going?"

She laughed unexpectedly. "We're always asking the same question. I guess it's because we're nervous. At least I am."

"You, Jess?"

"Ever since the avalanche."

"You shouldn't let yourself get superstitious about this mountain."

"Superstitious? Who said I'm superstitious? I was put off by the accident, that's all."

"Come on!" Howie shouted. "I've got a bomb-proof shelter up here."

As if disputing such a claim, the Witch's Fang loosed a rock from the cliffs above.

"Rock!" Jess yelled, automatically ducking and shielding her head with both arms.

An airborne fragment exploded into the snow directly behind her.

"I could hear it going past." Her face was white.

Todd tried to move, but his legs remained frozen.

Jess squeezed his hand. "Go on, Todd. Howie has a bombproof shelter up there."

A few minutes later Howie was reaching out and pulling them into a wide gap between the snow and the rock face.

"I was worried," he said. "I could hear the rockfall, but I couldn't see anything from here."

"Are we glad to see you," Jess said. "Have you got the sandwiches out? I need something to eat."

"Today's special is Swiss cheese on rye, open

face. Beverage is orange cooler with flecks of snow.
Table with a view, ma'am?" Howie gave her a big
hug.

"I wish I had your sense of humour, Howie.
That rock came so close I could hear it whistling
past my ear."

"Jeez — and I was sitting up here, being no help
whatsoever."

"Not much you could have done to help," Todd
said. "We were lucky."

"Come on, then — eat some of my sandwiches."

As they munched on Howie's sandwiches, a
single rock rumbled down the snow gully directly
to their right, spilled onto the snow slope and
disappeared into space.

"Well, I said we were bombproof here." Howie's
voice broke the silence.

As long as we stay put, Todd thought. The
trouble comes when we have to move.

"If Kurt couldn't handle this route ..." Jess
hesitated.

"Since when has Kurt become our touchstone
as far as climbing is concerned?" Todd said.

With the rockfall and the pain jabbing away at
his foot, Todd had almost forgotten Kurt. He could
picture him clawing his way to the summit, drinking in the clear mountain air, savouring the triumph of a first ascent. Damn it, Kurt didn't belong
in that picture. Did anyone else, for that matter?

Howie's voice jerked him back to the present.
"As I see it we have three options now."

"Options?" Jess repeated dubiously, eyeing the cliffs above them.

"We could continue up the snow, taking our chances with rockfall and hoping we can climb out of the gully higher up, or we could try to get onto the rock directly from here."

"And option number three?" Todd asked.

"We go back down and enjoy the beautiful sunny day."

"Putting option three aside, we'd certainly gain altitude fast in the gully."

Howie nodded.

"Whereas we could waste the rest of the day wandering along the base of the rock here, looking for a way up."

"Exactly."

Todd tilted his head back and surveyed the sheer cliffs above them. Everywhere was loose and crumbling rock, still greasy from the last snowfall. The difficulty, naturally, lay in even getting onto that rock. The horizontal gap where they were sitting was a metre or so deep with sheer walls behind. There was no good reason to believe that the melting action that had caused this would be different anywhere else. What if they had reached a dead end, as Jess had hinted? It was conceivable that Kurt had realized this and decided to give the north ridge a go.

"Under the circumstances," Howie said, "I'm leaning towards the gully. What do you say, Jess?"

"Maybe the danger from rockfall in the gully is

too great. What happened to option number three?"

"We're not discussing option number three," Todd broke in.

"The sun isn't into the gully yet and won't be for another half hour," Howie said. "With the temperature hovering around freezing, everything should be holding together."

"What about the rock that almost hit me, Howie?"

"A fluke. It probably came from the ridge."

Jess shook her head. "Some fluke. It felt like the Witch's Fang was out to get me."

"These things happen in the mountains," Howie said. "Of course I can't guarantee a hundred percent safety, but I'd say we have half an hour's good going in the gully."

"Translated, that means we have to make up our minds quickly," Jess added.

Howie nodded.

Todd swallowed the rest of his sandwich in one gulp.

"What are we waiting for?"

"Hold it, Todd. Jess?"

"I hate it when everything depends on me, Howie. Of course I'm going if you and Todd want to. I'm just not sure it's smart."

"I don't mind turning back."

"You do mind, Howie."

"Let's put it this way, Jess. I think it would be too bad to turn back before having a decent look at the gully. If we don't like what we find, we stop.

How's that?"

"You don't need to lecture me, Howie. I told you I'm coming."

"Sorry."

"Oh, forget it."

Todd stuffed his plastic water bottle and the remnants of lunch into his pack. Thanks to Howie, they were going on. They might have to turn back eventually, but not before giving Kurt a good run for the peak. From the next valley over, he heard the sound of a rockfall. Not yet midday and the sun was loosening things up. No doubt they would be hearing more of that ominous sound before the day was out. Pray it didn't come too close.

◇ CHAPTER 8

TODD CLAMBERED FROM THE GAP between the snow and rock face where they had taken refuge over lunch. Although their break had lasted only fifteen minutes, mind and body were sufficiently chilled that it was like starting the climb all over. Jess and Howie were standing outside, waiting to tie into the rope whenever he had it ready.

"Sorry to hold you up."

"If you hand me the rope, I'll untangle it," Howie offered.

"I can sort it out myself, Howie."

Todd struggled with the knot — a knot he had caused by pulling the wrong way — then watched as the coils came loose and slithered down the slope. He'd better be careful. Climbers had been known to drop their ropes in the stupidest places.

"Take your time," Howie told him.

Take your time — when every minute counted? True, the sun wasn't hitting the lower and upper reaches of the gully, but the mid-section, which was shallower and steeper, would soon be exposed, and in half an hour the whole gully would be a blinding shaft of sunlight. Better if Howie swore at him, told him to get off his butt.

"Are you ready to tie into the rope?" Jess asked. There was a slight edge to her voice.

"Half a minute, Jess." He fumbled with the carabiner, struggling to clip it into the nylon webbing of his climbing harness.

Nothing was working.

Howie tied a figure-eight knot in the climbing rope and handed it over. "You get to go last this time, Todd. Lucky man — nothing to do but relax and watch us struggling."

Being the last person ready was aggravating. As Todd clipped his carabiner into the knot, he could feel Howie and Jess watching his every move.

"With crampons on, we can skip the belaying and move together," Howie was saying. "Everyone take a few coils and stay close. Okay?"

They paused beside the gap, every sense alert to the slightest sound from above. Only the distant whirring of a waterfall and snow slumping underfoot broke the silence. Was the Witch's Fang holding back, savouring a moment of calm, before they committed themselves to her gully?

Don't be crazy, Todd told himself. You're letting your imagination take over. You're beginning to sound like Jess. Somewhere far above them, the

Witch's Fang seemed to shift imperceptibly in the shimmering sunlight.

"Now," Howie said quietly. And they left the sheltering rock face and stepped into the gully.

Todd shook his head. Had they sacrificed safety for the sake of speed? If they moved singly and belayed each other, they'd take forever. Besides, where could you set up a decent belay? There was nothing except the occasional rock protruding from a thin covering of snow. No, in such a gully, safety and speed were linked.

Todd winced as his left crampon tipped him sideways. Watch it — slab of bare rock below. He paused to catch his breath and pick up the coils of rope he'd dropped.

Don't look down, he reminded himself.

Now he had to hurry to catch up with Jess who was climbing fast. Her breath was rising in the crystal air, and he could imagine the steady sound of her breathing — in and out, in and out ... His own was rasping. The rope between them grew taut. Only one coil left to drop — too tight and it could upset her balance.

"Slow down," he called at last.

Jess turned around. His own fear was mirrored in her eyes. "We have to hurry, Todd. The sun is starting to hit the steeper section ahead."

"I'm into hard stuff," Howie warned. "I don't like this thin plating of ice and snow, but it'll go." His usually upbeat voice sounded subdued.

Todd didn't trust the surface either. What if the

ice sloughed off? He felt each step carefully, nudged his crampons farther in where possible. Rocks just below the surface. But worst of all was the sunlight he saw looming ahead. Jess was already there, her loose hair streaming from her helmet like a halo.

Jeez, I'm scared, Todd thought. Better admit it. Everything feels numb, my brain included. Before the accident this would have been a breeze, I think. But I'm not sure any more.

"What's up?" Todd felt a sudden pull on his climbing harness.

Howie and Jess were stopped below a rock outcrop, taking in his rope. The pressure on his climbing harness was welcome. Sam would call it a psychological belay, meaning it felt good but was technically useless. So what, if he was climbing more safely. Todd stopped beside the others and wiped the sweat from his forehead.

"Gradually warming up," Howie was quick to comment. "How are you doing? That gnarly section reminded me of our Mt. Slesse climb."

"Yeah."

"You all right, Todd?"

"Sure, I'm fine." He took a closer look at the rock blocking their way. No way around, except over. Not what he needed.

"I didn't want to tackle this next section before you were here," Howie explained. "Too much loose rock. The going will be easier above."

"What about the rock right here?" Jess asked. "To get onto it you need a gorilla reach, which is fine for you and Todd ..."

"No prob," Howie insisted. "One tricky move at the beginning and that's it."

"Howie, your one tricky move is beyond my reach."

"I really meant no prob, Jess. Todd will give you a boost." Howie turned his attention to the rock.

"No prob ... it's always no prob," Jess grumbled.

"I'd like a belay going over this rock," Howie said.

"That will definitely be a problem," Jess said, wrapping the rope around the shaft of her ice axe.

"Do the best you can."

"Nope, it won't work, Howie. I can't get my ice axe far enough in."

"What about your ice screws?" Todd asked.

"Don't you remember? Too much stuff to lug around. We left them behind. Typical, eh, when you need something."

Jess had moved to the left side of the gully, which was more sheltered from the sun. "The snow is better here."

"Good," Howie said, "because we haven't time to mess around."

"Hold it, Jess. I'll ram my ice axe in too," Todd offered.

As Howie bent over to take off his crampons, he scraped one hand across the surface and let the granular ice crystals sift through his fingers. "See? Before long it'll be slush and we need to be gone."

"I can't do more than hurry," Jess told him.

"And you aren't going anywhere before I rig up a half-decent belay."

"Sorry, didn't mean to nag you, Jess. But we're in a tight spot here. Stay close to the gully wall in case I drop any rocks. Can I go yet?"

"On belay," Jess said glumly.

Todd watched as Howie, with a few swings of his ice axe, enlarged the platform he was standing on. What incredible balance the guy had! From there he could reach the top of the rock with his right arm, keeping a downward pressure with the left. Not much to grasp on to. But that didn't matter, because with both legs spread-eagled across the surface he was able to worm his way up.

Pray that the whole chunk doesn't come loose, Todd thought. And try to remember what he's doing. Your turn is coming.

"I'm over it," Howie called. "I'll keep going until I find a decent belay place."

"You have about ten metres of rope left," Jess told him.

Silence, except for the steady swish of snow granules over rock. The warmth of the sun soaked through their clothes and into their skin. Normally, it would have felt comforting, but warmth was the last thing they needed now.

"You can come!" Howie shouted. "There's lots of good firm snow up here. And I've got you on a bombproof belay."

Todd's breathing eased back to normal. Good old Howie. You couldn't climb with a better guy.

"Ready, Jess?" Standing on Howie's platform, Todd cupped his hands at waist height and braced himself for her weight.

"You're sure I'm not too heavy?"

"A mere featherweight."

"Climbing," she called up to Howie.

Todd watched her rope until she had cleared the rock bulge, then bent down to take off his crampons. Now he'd be ready when Jess called. But could he handle this rock with his rotten foot? Easy for Jess and Howie to spread-eagle and worm their way up.

Hey, Todd, one step at a time, he reminded himself.

Hadn't he spent the past ten months or so listening to that refrain from doctors, nurses, physios, parents, friends? One step at a time. Eventually those words were absorbed through his skin, becoming part of a persistent inner voice.

First step: out of hospital and into a temporary cast. Then in a wheelchair or hobbling around with crutches. Wiped after a single city block, arms and shoulders screaming for a rest.

Second step: crutches gone and cane in their place. Shuffling like an old man. One step at a time, remember?

Third step: riding a bike for the very first time. Fresh air eddying, wheels turning, the whole earth suddenly moving. Mobility.

"You may never walk in the mountains again, Todd."

Whose voice was that? He didn't care. He didn't have to listen to them any more. He'd learned his lines — one step at a time, one step.

Fourth step: I think I'm taking it now. And if so, I need to keep repeating my lines. More than ever I need to keep repeating my lines. One step at a time ...

"Todd, I'm up with Howie. You can come."

"Be with you shortly."

There was comfort in the rope — the unspoken connection. He followed Jess and Howie's example, reaching one arm up and stretching his legs across the rock surface. It was easy. He could feel his body arching over the rock bulge in the old familiar way, his legs providing the momentum.

As Todd moved up he could see Jess and Howie waiting for him where the gully ended abruptly in a rock face. A cinch to there, but then what?

"It's dicey," Howie was saying, "but thanks to this vertical line of harder rock, I think it will go." He took hold of an angular chunk protruding from the dike and it fell out like a cupboard drawer and took off down the gully. "Um, as long as nobody pulls on anything."

Todd watched the boulder gather speed as it tumbled, turning end over end like some lopsided projectile, before launching itself into space. He could feel his stomach churning as he watched the airy passage. They might well have been standing below when such a chunk came.

"Did you have to drop that boulder, Howie? Couldn't you have put it somewhere?"

"Yeah, you tell me where. Besides it's fun trundling boulders when you're sure nobody is below."

"You can never be too sure, Howie."

"Come off it, Todd. You know Kurt isn't there."

Granted. But what would the Witch's Fang say to three young upstarts rolling boulders down her flanks? Would it prompt her to follow suit? No, Howie should have found some other home for that boulder. Todd stared down the gully until he had to look away.

"I'll take the lead," Howie announced. "And I promise not to trundle any boulders, okay?" He added several pitons and his piton hammer to the chocks and carabiners already clipped into his nylon shoulder strap.

"Go easy," Jess cautioned him.

"You should be leading, Jess. You're the rock jock here, but we're already tied into the rope. Hope you don't mind."

"Mind? Go on, Howie, I'm grateful."

Where the gully met the rock face, Howie had hacked out a platform large enough for two people to stand. Todd braced himself, then rammed his ice axe into the snow and wrapped Howie's rope around the shaft. For good measure he stomped on it until only the head was showing. In case of a fall, it would prevent Howie from taking off down the gully. But to protect himself as he climbed higher, Howie would have to insert a chock or hammer in a piton, to which he could attach his rope. A running belay, it was called — another of Sam's favourite terms. Todd knew his spiel by heart. If in doubt, use a running belay. If still in doubt, use two or three running belays. You'll fall only past your last chock or piton.

For a few minutes they could hear Howie struggling directly overhead — boots scratching against rock, the metallic clang of his climbing hardware, a few muffled curses, followed by a single rock screaming overhead and splashing into the gully below. Trouble, or part of Howie's route-clearing efforts? Was he calling? Without thinking, Todd leaned out to get a glimpse of the action above.

Jess shoved him against the gully wall. "Are you crazy? You'll get hit."

"I thought I heard Howie calling."

They both listened, but the only sound was their own breathing and the wind swirling off the ridge. A single raven hung effortlessly over them, riding the updrafts.

"Awfully quiet, isn't it?" Todd whispered.

"I know, and with every little sound echoing from the gully walls, it's impossible to tell where he is."

Todd braced himself against the rock and gripped Howie's rope more firmly. A slight tremor on the line was followed by a sharp upward pull.

Some delicate move taking place overhead? If so, it was crucial not to place any extra drag on Howie's rope. Seconds later, the clear metallic ring of a piton hammer reverberated between the gully walls.

"He must be confident the rock is solid."

"Either that or he's desperate to tie himself in somewhere, Jess."

"I have yet to see Howie desperate on a climb. He doesn't push himself beyond his limits. Leave that to Kurt."

She would have to mention Kurt. The rope jerked again and Todd let more slack run through his hands.

"I wonder what Howie's up to?" His words were drowned out by an explosion from above. Instinctively, Todd flattened himself against the rock and covered his head. The rock barrage hit the snow a metre or so below their platform and bounded into space with the ease of a slow-motion sequence. Silence hung in the air afterwards, a silence as ominous as the initial crack. Todd stared at the dark cliffs looming above the gully. Although the final spire of the Witch's Fang was still invisible from their present perch, she was obviously making her presence known.

"I'm glad I wasn't climbing," was all Jess said.

"The rope might have set it off, Jess. Don't move. Maybe there's more coming."

What had he gotten them into? And what was he trying to prove? That he was the same Todd

Rushton as before the accident? Well, he wasn't, not by a long shot.

"Hullo?" came the echo of Howie's voice. "Are you all right down there? All right down there?"

"We're okay," Todd called back.

"He'll pick up the echo at least."

"Be quiet, Jess. Let's listen." Another tug came on the rope. "That's it — there's no more slack. He must want you to come."

"Well, he'll have to wait a minute. I'm too tensed up to climb safely."

Todd watched as she circled her arms overhead and took a few deep breaths before making her first move. Glide was the more appropriate word, Todd thought. If only he looked like that.

A few minutes later there was nothing left of Jess's presence apart from a shaking in the rope. He was alone. Little to do except watch her rope, wait his turn and hope no rocks came barrelling down. He remembered one time with Sam ... Uh-oh, focus on the present. The past was not his concern, at least not when Jess needed his help.

There was only a metre of slack left in the rope.

"Nearing the end, Jess."

He ought to have warned her earlier. What she didn't need was a sudden jerk. Half a metre left. No choice — she had to find a place to stop.

Her voice drifted down. "... with Howie. Come now ..." At least that's what it sounded like.

The rope attached to his harness tightened and began to exert pressure against his ribs. Damnit!

Howie and Jess were taking in the few remaining centimetres of slack, presuming he was already climbing. They knew better than to hold him that tight. Still stiff from standing hunched against the rock, Todd lurched up and pulled the rope. He needed space. His balance was lousy enough as it was.

"Climbing!" he yelled. Obviously they didn't hear or weren't listening. The rope was dragging on his harness.

Concentrate, Todd told himself. Don't let anger take over. This narrow rib of rock dissolving into sky was his pathway. Somewhere up there Jess and Howie were pulling on his rope ... way too hard, damn it. Forget it. Focus on the rock.

Todd's hands slid across the surface, feeling for texture, any slight irregularities. His fingertips curled over a knob. He moved up. Geologically interesting, this dike — an ancient volcanic vent that congealed before it reached the surface — now a distinct line, obviously more erosion resistant than the surrounding rock. And as Howie had already demonstrated, reasonably secure unless you pulled it outward.

Todd's boots found the leverage he had been seeking and his fingers located the next minute indentation to propel his body upwards. The pitch was near his limit. If he lingered too long in any one stance, his calf muscles turned to jelly. Another upward glide. The familiar rhythm was taking over. Easy, he told himself, don't start scrambling for bombproof handholds, because there aren't any. Use the legs, the feet, and let the fingers do the delicate work. The black cliffs above and the angular blocks of the gully below began to distance themselves, leaving only the immediate rock to focus on and the smooth, rhythmic dance. And as long as he didn't miss a beat everything would be okay …

A chock appeared at eye level, wedged into a crack. Why hadn't Jess removed it? When Todd pulled on the chock, it slipped out effortlessly and tumbled into the gully below. He shook his head. The chock had been Howie's safety margin; his rope had been attached to it, and in case of a slip that same chock should have prevented him from falling. But the ease with which it came loose made Todd's hand tingle.

"Rock!" a voice from above shouted.

A boulder, no doubt dislodged by his own rope, bounded past. Half-audible curses from Howie.

"Can you hold it a second?" Howie asked. "I've got to shift my belay position away from this loose junk."

"Make it snappy, Howie. I'm standing on a sloping rock knob."

His foot was throbbing painfully. If only there was a decent handhold somewhere. He could feel sweat greasing his palms as they groped over the rock. Smooth. Absolutely nothing there. Both legs were shaking. Panic gripped him — he couldn't hold on much longer. One foot slipping, hands flailing ... This was it — he was falling ...

"HOWIE!"

The sudden jerk flung Todd against the rock. He found himself hanging from the rope a metre or so below his last position. Howie was talking to him.

"Sorry for the excitement. Everything's under control up here. I've got you on a bombproof belay. You see my rope ladder ahead? From there it's a walk to the ridge."

"Oh, sure, just a walk." Nevertheless, he could feel Howie's mesmeric drawl relaxing him, slowing down his heartbeat.

Directly above him lay the obstacle, a slight outward curve of the dike with no obvious route around. Thank god for Howie's persistence. Somehow he had managed to bang in a piton while balancing on a dicey rock flake and suspend a rope ladder from the piton. As long as the pull was straight down, it was solid, Todd figured. He slipped his left foot into the lowest rung. Whew! Taking the pressure off eased the pain considerably. With one free hand Todd wiped the condensation from his dark glasses. It sure helped if you could see!

"Don't forget my rope ladder." The voice couldn't be more than a few metres away, but Howie himself was invisible.

"Forgetting your rope ladder is the least of my worries, Howie."

"It's my best homemade ladder."

"It better be," Todd muttered. He eased his

other foot onto the lowest rung and felt the ropes squeezing painfully. "Time out," he called up. Had the piton shifted slightly with his weight? Or was his imagination playing tricks again?

Todd slipped his left foot off the ladder and let it dangle freely. For a moment he shut his eyes and forced himself to breathe regularly and deeply. The pain diminished. A light breeze moved across the rock face, pivoting the ladder with his attached form. "When the wind blows the cradle will rock ... and down will come ..."

Todd jerked his eyes open. With one hand grasping the top rung, he climbed up. He was now eye level with the piton. Two more rungs to go, but first he had to find a substantial handhold. A finger crack half a metre up — it should do. Now unclip Howie's precious rope ladder as he went by.

"Sacrifice the piton," Howie told him.

"Exactly what I aim to do, Howie. It'll make a great foothold."

Howie and Jess were belaying him from the ridge. In a few minutes he would be with them, having his first close-up view of the Witch's Fang. So why hesitate? Todd glanced back. If those rock-strewn cliffs, the gully and even the snow fields far below were pockmarked by her changing moods, what would it be like higher up?

✧ CHAPTER 9

"TERRIFIC PANT-SHREDDING COUNTRY," Howie observed.

"Understatement," Jess replied.

Where they were sitting the ridge was less than a metre wide. Todd dragged himself into a standing position and pivoted slowly around, trying to absorb the panorama. Yes, it was clearly a Howie understatement.

Ahead was a jagged, knife-edged ridge, dropping three hundred to four hundred metres on either side. Suffice to say it was a long way down. A raven, perhaps the same bird he had noticed earlier, skimmed the ridge, rode an updraft to the summit and then sheered off into the valley.

"It's your country," Todd whispered. "I wish we could do the same.

And the summit itself? An extinguished flame, a black decaying tooth, spiralling upwards. All the old images came back to haunt him. The Witch's

Fang — formed by fire and ice, ice and fire ... Who knows which came first or when?

Howie clapped him on the back. "Don't let the scenery get you down, Todd. You know what happens — a ridge or a face that looks awesome from a distance opens up as you come closer."

"There are exceptions, Howie."

"Very few in my experience. You always find hidden gullies, ledges, chimneys or something."

Jess passed along the bag of trail mix. "Howie and I have been munching. You better too, while there's room to sit and be comfortable."

"Thanks, Jess." Not that he felt especially hungry.

"Does anyone else want to take the lead?" Howie asked.

Todd surveyed the ridge line, trying to erase the drop on either side. Was he up to it? A moment's hesitation.

And Jess barged in. "I'll take over."

His sister — pushy as usual. Still, she had saved him from making a tough decision. "Are you sure, Jess?"

"I said I'd take the lead."

Of course. He sensed the annoyance in her voice.

"Then go for it," Howie said, grabbing her around the waist and setting her down on his far side.

"Careful," Jess protested.

"I was thinking about the woman who came along on a club trip last summer. Remember how she freaked out on a harmless little ridge, grabbed me around the waist and almost pulled us off the mountain?"

"And seeing me here reminds you of her, I suppose. Gee, thanks a lot, Howie. If it was a man I bet you'd be telling the story differently."

"I can't help it if she was a woman. Do you need some carabiners?"

"Admit it, Howie, you're a chauvinist. Yes, I need two more 'biners."

"I'm not a chauvinist."

"Yes, you are. Watch my rope, please. I'm starting on."

Give them a few minutes to cool down, Todd decided. As their argument jangled along the ridge and the distance between them increased, his thoughts collapsed inward. He couldn't help wondering if Kurt was still pressing his luck on the other side of the mountain.

He remembered once when Kurt was leading a party and refused to turn back even though he could see a storm coming. Thanks to him, they'd been caught on the mountain as clouds surged around and the electricity in the air set their ice axes ringing. And what had Kurt done? Instead of crouching below the ridge like everyone else, he'd stood there celebrating the storm like some crazed mountain demon. By all the laws of science or superstition he ought to have been struck down.

Todd felt the rope sliding through his hands. "Can you give me another metre?" Howie called. "If so, I can reach a good belay point."

As Todd moved forward to give Howie some slack, his boot scuffed a rock loose.

Trust no hold on the Witch's Fang. His father's familiar incantation returned. Forget your hands, place your feet cautiously — less danger then of dislodging rocks. So what could you trust on this knobbly backbone of a ridge? Not very much.

Todd's rope tightened. "Should I come?" he asked.

"Okay, on belay."

That was their only connection now — a tension running through the rope, a continual easing off and pulling in. No space for chatter. But friends for life are made here, Todd thought, and enemies too, perhaps. He reached up and caught the end of Howie's boot, the one firm point on an otherwise crumbling ridge. "Not the best technique," Howie observed with a smile, "but I'm glad to provide a little stability."

"You do, Howie, believe me, you do."

Jess flashed them a victory sign from farther up the ridge.

"I'd rate this next pitch as moderate class five," Howie said, "and on rotten rock that's no piece of cake. I hope I do as well as Jess."

"Take care, Howie."

"Don't worry, I always do."

Todd watched his friend straddling the narrow ridge — one foot on each side, as Jess had done before him. *À cheval*, or on horseback, as Sam always liked to describe it. But where the rock began the next upward spiral, this became impossible. Now comes the dicey section, Todd thought. Howie was testing each foothold, each handhold — never relying on a single point. Even so, falling rock marked his progress.

Gradually Howie's form became blurred in the shimmering heat waves that were rising and then dissolving into the cooler air above the ridge. Jess was somewhere among the shifting rock pinnacles, belaying Howie. Come together. Separate. Come together again. Separate. Pull the rope in. Let the rope out — the constant repetition of climbing. Soon Howie would be with Jess. Then he would follow. Like pilgrims creeping towards a shrine they came. But even pilgrims must look away from the sky blue of an ever-receding horizon and concentrate on the ground beneath.

"Damn!" was all Howie said when a rock, loosened by the rope above, smashed down on his hand.

Todd looked up to see Howie clutching his hand and Jess bending over him. No make-believe pilgrim stuff. This was real. He could feel the adrenaline surge dragging him forward, heedless of the knife-edged ridge, the crumbling rock, until Jess shouted. "Wait. Let me belay you up, Todd. We don't need another accident."

Another accident? He hadn't been thinking of accidents, only of Howie.

When Todd reached them on the ledge, Howie

looked at him and apologized. "Chunk of rock got the back of my hand. I wasn't paying attention. I should have been watching for rockfall."

"It wasn't your fault, Howie. Everything is loose. That's why no one has climbed the mountain."

"Help me, Todd. Get the rope out of my way." Jess tore open some bandages and pressed them over the wound. A few seconds later blood was staining the gauze, and Howie's face was pale against the rock.

"The bleeding won't stop, even with pressure," Jess whispered. "And we're stuck here without help. What if he goes into shock?"

"Let me hold the bandage, Jess."

The warm flow stuck to the palm of his hand, and the ragged line of bone pressed against his own flesh, making him feel ill.

"How long should I keep holding?"

"Until the bleeding stops, obviously. Put your scarf over top if you have to. Anything will do. This is what happens when you tackle too dangerous a mountain."

Too dangerous a mountain. An accident and his best friend gets hurt. His fault. The words oozed through his mind like the blood through the bandage, causing Todd to increase his pressure on the hand.

Howie winced. "Easy, something's broken there."

"You're pressing way too hard," Jess complained.

"Give me his hand. You can dig out some painkillers from the first-aid kit."

"No way." Howie shook his head. "I'm not doping myself up and falling asleep here. It's too dangerous."

"Howie, you have to take some painkillers. Your hand will start throbbing and you'll feel worse later on."

"I feel better with you holding my hand, Jess."

"You're hopeless."

"I know. I've really gone and messed things up."

Todd draped an arm around his friend's shoulder. "It's not your fault, Howie. I pressured you into coming. I'm the one who should be apologizing."

"I was careless. I wasn't watching. Jeez, what an idiot!"

"Howie, stop apologizing and swallow these pills." Jess stuffed the capsules into his mouth. "And don't feel guilty. The accident happened; it wasn't anyone's fault."

"I need water or something else to wash down these monster pills," Howie gasped.

Jess held out the water bottle. "Drink as much as you can and try to relax, Howie." She draped her down jacket around his shoulders. "Warm enough?"

"Yes, but I won't fall asleep. We have to decide what's next."

"What's next is resting here until the bleeding stops," Jess told him. "You can't go anywhere for a while; it would be too dangerous. That much I do know."

"Then if we're sitting around here because of me, you should go on."

"What do you mean?" Todd asked.

"Go to the top, you idiot. It isn't far."

"Howie, you must be out of your mind. Jess and I are staying here, looking after you."

"I thought you wanted to climb the Witch's Fang. The chance comes along and what happens? You blow it."

"I did want to climb the Witch's Fang, but ..."

"Climbing the Witch's Fang isn't the big issue now," Jess broke in.

"It's important for Todd, or at least I think it is." Howie closed his eyes. "Jeez, I'm too tired ... whatever, to cope with you Rushtons."

"We have to tie him in," Todd whispered. "If he goes to sleep, he could fall off."

"Tie him to what?"

"I don't know. Hold on to him while I look around."

Howie's head drooped and swayed onto Jess's shoulder.

Todd followed the ridge line to where the black decaying rock flared into the final spire — less than an hour away if a person was lucky. Don't even think about it. The summit didn't matter now. What mattered was the ledge underneath them, barely a metre wide, room for three people and not much more. But if they had to stop it was the best, possibly the only, place on an otherwise steep and broken ridge. Todd ran his fingers over the rock, feeling for cracks or indentations where he could insert a chock.

"As I suspected, everything is too loose. What I'll have to do is place a piton in the back corner of the ledge where the rock looks more solid."

"When you mess around with pitons, isn't there a danger of setting off a rockfall?" Jess wondered.

"Howie needs to be tied in. We have to take that risk. If you can think of anything better ..."

When Howie heard his name, he stirred. "No prob. Except I'm sleepy."

Todd patted him on the shoulder. "As soon as we have you tied in, Howie, you can have a snooze."

"Don't want to sleep here," Howie muttered.

Todd reached over and unclipped the hammer and remaining pitons from Howie's climbing harness. "Don't worry when you hear the hammering," he said quietly.

At the first hammer crack, Howie sat up. "Jeez, you could have warned me. What are you trying to do, bring down the mountain?"

"Tying you in, Howie." Todd attached a sling to the piton, then ran it through Howie's climbing harness. "There, now you can relax."

"Yeah, I'll relax for a few minutes. But don't let me go to sleep. We need to decide ..." His voice trailed off again.

Todd turned to Jess. "At least he can't fall now. Has the bleeding stopped?"

"Mostly." Jess uncovered Howie's hand. "Take

a look."

Todd forced himself to look at the whiteness of the exposed bone. "How's he ever going to climb down?"

Jess shrugged. "Initially I didn't think about anything except stopping the bleeding and preventing shock. But now ... what are we going to do, Todd?"

"We'll figure something out. Listen, Jess, I'm sorry for bringing you here. It's all my fault. I knew the dangers, but I was set on coming."

"I wanted to come. Howie wanted to come. Nobody dragged us here. And apologizing won't get us down."

"I know. Just let me think." Todd checked his watch. Almost five o'clock and it was a mighty long way down. Haze was drifting in from the west and forming a broken halo around the sun. He shaded his eyes and stared at the sundogs. An ominous sign, forerunners of a weather change, perhaps?

"We should consider climbing down," Jess said finally. "There's light until nine o'clock."

"We could never make it all the way, and once into the gully there's no stopping. And what about Howie, drowsy from the painkillers?"

She frowned. "And what if his hand swells up, gets worse overnight?

"I'm not thrilled about bivouacking here either, but the alternative seems worse." Todd glanced towards the west again. As long as their weather held ...

Clouds were building over the horizon. Gold-fringed by the sun, they looked harmless enough at the moment, but who knew what the long hours of darkness might bring? Already there was a different tinge to the air.

"Do you think there's a front coming in?" Jess asked, voicing his own concerns.

"Most likely end-of-the-day haze," he said, trying to sound optimistic, though when he checked his altimeter, it was down from the morning.

"I'd hate to be stuck here in bad weather," Jess went on. "Can you imagine what it would be like having snow, or even rain, here?"

Trouble was, he could. "I didn't exactly choose this location, Jess."

"Maybe we should talk to Howie, see what he thinks about going down."

"I doubt he's in any shape to voice an opinion."

Howie's head was slumped over his knees. Jess shook his shoulders gently and asked, "Should we try moving you?"

"Huh? Oh sure, try moving. Still time to reach the top." He struggled to lift his head, then relaxed again.

"You're right, Todd. We couldn't go down now with Howie even if we wanted."

"So what's next, Jess?"

"Don't ask me. Except I'll try to figure out the best way to bandage Howie's hand for the way down tomorrow."

"You should put on a sweater, Jess. The air is

cooling off. Take mine for now."

"Thanks. I'd hardly noticed." She shaded her eyes against the sun. "Better enjoy the sun while we can, because tonight will be cool."

"Anything I can do to help, Jess?"

"Not really. Eventually we'll need something to eat, and then we'll have the fun of arranging ourselves for the night."

"I'm not looking forward to that either."

Todd checked his watch again. Five-thirty. Still enough time to make the top, not that he was considering it.

"Why do you think Howie keeps rambling on about the summit?" he asked.

"Because he feels bad about the accident."

"He shouldn't."

"That's Howie for you. Also, he imagines himself in your shoes, within shouting distance of the top, almost."

A rockfall somewhere nearby interrupted their conversation. With the sound echoing all around them, it was impossible to pinpoint the location. A sizable one — that's all Todd knew.

Howie opened his eyes and smiled when he saw Todd. "Back from the climb, eh? Good. Rockfall came from higher up. Afraid you were involved." After struggling to continue, he let his head sink back onto Jess's shoulder.

"Whew," Todd whistled. "He's drifting after taking those painkillers, but he still manages to slot me into his dreamworld."

After the rumble had died away, it was as if nothing had happened. It was always like that in the mountains, Todd mused. Whether it was an ice bridge collapsing, rock falling, ice slumping from a glacier snout, a cornice breaking off — it didn't matter what cataclysmic disturbance — always the vast, indifferent silence of the mountain returned.

"For a moment I thought our whole ridge was going," Jess whispered.

"Maybe Howie's remote hearing is more accurate than ours. He seemed to think the rockfall came from the top somewhere. Wonder what could have caused it?"

Kurt ... but Todd didn't mention the fleeting thought. Could Kurt possibly be at or near the top and having difficulties?

Todd let his gaze wander up the ridge and onto the peak. It looked tantalizingly close. Wait a minute — was he imagining a shape, something moving up there? It was probably just the sun's slanting rays playing over the summit block, but it sure looked like a figure bending over a half-built cairn.

"Darn it all, Jess, I'm wondering whether one of us shouldn't go for the top as Howie keeps suggesting. We could also check on Kurt."

"Not me. I'm looking after Howie, and I'm not going anywhere but down."

"Positive? I could look after Howie and you go up."

"Do I have to put it in writing, as you always tell me, Todd? I'm staying with Howie."

"What would you say if I was to go?"

"You would be alone. I'd say you need to ask yourself what that means — not down in the valley or in the city, but here, right now. Then you decide whether to go."

"But what do *you* think, Jess? Should I go or not?"

"I don't know. How could I? I wish you wouldn't keep asking me. You've climbed alone often enough."

"I know, but it's not the same." Alone, solo, unaccompanied. No matter which word Todd chose, the notion of climbing the Witch's Fang by himself ended in fear. The idea was crazy. There had been too many close calls already.

"I'm not going, Jess. You need my help."

"Don't worry about me. I can manage fine."

"You don't want help with dinner or anything?"

"Dinner? All we have is soup, rye crisp and cheese. I've got hours to heat the soup water."

"Are you saying that I should go?"

"No, I'm saying you have to decide."

"I would take the light climbing rope, some slings, carabiners, a few chocks and pitons, not much else. By myself I'd be quick. And the danger from rock fall would be minimal."

"I'm beginning to think Howie was right about your going."

"Thanks, Jess. If I don't like the look of it, if I

feel unsafe, I'll turn back. I promise."

Howie woke to the commotion. "Jeez, I thought you'd gone and come back. Now you seem to be going. Take my rope ladder," he mumbled.

"Thanks, Howie, I will. I can hardly hear what you're saying." Todd bent closer to listen.

"Don't trust any hold ..." Howie's words trailed off.

Strange to hear Sam's familiar words echoing from Howie. Trust no hold on the Witch's Fang.

"You take care too, Howie."

"We'll have some warm soup waiting," Jess promised.

"See you later. If I do make it to the top, I won't be lingering there."

✧ CHAPTER 10

TODD GLANCED BACK at the two figures huddled together on the ledge. He was directly above them — any clumsy move or miscalculation on his part could dislodge a rock. Jess turned and gave him a wave. In a few moments they would be beyond sight or sound range and he would be effectively cut off from them. Alone.

On each side of him tongues of snow lapped at the ridge — chutes to the valley — three hundred or more metres straight down. He was out of shape, climbing awkwardly, having to use his hands when it wasn't necessary. And his foot hurt. This was as good a spot as any to turn around and admit defeat. Ahead the going looked rough.

Then stop. Turn around.

Todd shut his eyes and leaned against the rock, anything to blot out the emptiness overtaking him. But there was no escape — closing his eyes only made him dizzy. The whole mountain seemed to be shifting and flowing away beneath his feet. He squeezed the rock with both hands until his body stopped shaking and everything grew still. Not quite. His friend the raven was drawing spirals in the sapphire air above, then drifting down to spread the news of solitary splendour — the peaks and cornices, glaciers and ice caves, the distant, shining sea.

You're right. It is incredible.

There was no reason to turn, not yet. Panic had gripped him, shaken him for an instant and robbed him of his senses. When the danger was real, when it was unsafe to go on, he would know.

Directly ahead and blocking the way was a gendarme, a narrow spire of rock which he somehow had to bypass. That meant moving off the ridge and onto the actual face of the mountain. A gust of wind rustled his jacket. Not exactly what he needed when the going was airy!

Take it easy, he told himself. The familiar climber's dialogue that provided the rhythm for his forward progress was starting to take over. Meaningless jargon to anybody else, perhaps, but it was his own proven prescription. "One step at a time, remember? Focus on the problem. Which problem? The gendarme and how to get around it."

Todd pulled a couple of slings from his pack and tied them together. A butterfly knot should do the trick. Now came the tricky part — crawling up on the gendarme as if he was stalking some wild animal and finally snaring the top with his sling.

Not bad. He managed to loop it around the rocky spire on his first throw.

Todd exerted some pressure on the sling. Solid enough. Now with the extra safety it provided, he could afford to move onto the face. Careful. A definite lack of holds there and the drop was more or less straight down. "Don't commit yourself to one hold. Two is good; three improves the odds. Watch out — a chunk breaking loose. Free falling and no sound as it drops, because everything is vertical. Eerie silence. The firmness of the sling feels good."

"Got to get going, got to get going ..." Todd heard himself whispering the long-ago words that he used to sing while trying to keep up with his father. And here he was, years later, still mumbling the same old song.

As Todd pulled himself back onto the ridge, a whiff of alpine fir drifted up with the same wind that was rustling his jacket. Homesick. He was suddenly homesick for everyone — the two figures huddled on the ledge, Leo down below, Sam and Norma even farther away. How were they all doing without him?

The final spire of the Witch's Fang rose above him, blotting out the evening sky. It became a knife point aimed at his heart because balancing there on the hilt was something that looked like ...

It couldn't be, but yes, it was Kurt Stone.

Todd could see his figure, bending over to place another rock on the cairn he was building. At any moment Kurt might call down to him, saying the north ridge was a piece of cake, the view was great and that he ought to come up. He could feel Kurt grinning. Well, he wasn't going up. No way he'd share the summit with him. He would rather go back down. Who cared about summit bagging?

Before turning around, Todd forced himself to look up again. It was then he realized his mistake and started laughing hysterically. His "Kurt Stone" was the same rock formation he had mistaken for a figure from down below, only this time from a different angle and much closer. Contorted by fire and ice, it was a perfect crouching climber. Kurt Stone, frozen forever in time.

Buoyed up by his laughter, Todd surveyed the final tower — a thin wedge of rock, exposed to the elements and eroded to bare bone and definitely more solid looking than the ridge below. Extreme. What else could one say? Above him, but well beyond reach, was a narrow chimney that dwindled into a crack higher up. Impossible to see farther. The chimney was the key, all right — if he could only get there. No problem if he was on level ground — he'd simply push himself to the limits and boulder his way up, knowing he couldn't fall more than a metre or so. But here, alone and on loose rock, with incredible exposure, he knew his choice was difficult.

Todd checked his watch. He had been gone half an hour.

Already the sun's lengthening shadows were

playing over the rock face, making it difficult to distinguish features. The surface texture was fading. Maybe this is it, Todd thought. I promised Jess that I would turn back if I didn't feel comfortable.

Wait a second. Above his head there was an indentation running diagonally across the rock. He curled his fingers over the rim. It was deeper than he thought. But could he trust his weight to it without a belay or aid of any kind? His hands pressed against the roughness of the rock. Solid enough. There was nothing substantial for his feet though, other than the friction of the rock surface — nowhere he could insert a chock. Yet directly above him was the narrow chimney and possibly easy going to the very top. Choices. He wished Howie was there to say "No prob, man."

Todd felt his fingers tightening over the indentation. As long as the pull was straight down, the risk of anything coming loose diminished. Finger power — that's what rock climbing was all about. Finger power — he could feel it working, allowing him to move his feet a little higher. He could almost reach the chimney. Just a few more centimetres.

Todd's whole body was trembling from the exertion, and sweat dotted his forehead. If he could get his hands into that chimney ... And if he couldn't? You don't think those thoughts, Todd. You empty your mind and climb. When there is no easy turning back, you don't wait around until muscles are exhausted and the mind is numb. You go up those few remaining centimetres. With both hands Todd grasped the side of the chimney and, leaning back slightly, walked his feet onto the indentation. Now he was high enough to wedge his shoulders into the chimney.

For a moment Todd hung there, letting his breathing return to normal. He'd love to hear Howie describing such a pitch. "Hey, it was radical, man. Especially that partial layback into the chimney. Spilled some sweat there, eh?" Whatever, he would have lots to tell Howie later on.

Although the way ahead looked reasonably clear, Todd knew it wouldn't be easy. This wasn't the classic-style chimney that allowed you to brace feet and back against opposing walls and simply walk up. Here the chimney was too narrow. All he could do was wedge himself in and squirm up, like some ungainly beetle.

"Aah!" Todd couldn't silence the sharp cry as his left foot felt the stress of the upward motion.

A chockstone wedged in the chimney ahead looked bombproof, so why not keep going and get the climb over with?

"Hold on." Maybe time was running out, but he could afford to take a closer look, possibly run a sling around the chockstone and fashion a running belay of sorts.

"If in doubt, hang a belay." Todd could hear his father saying the familiar words.

Great, he'd actually managed to get a sling around the chockstone, and with some effort he could tie himself in, using the lighter climbing rope he had brought along. A running belay — Sam would approve, all right. Besides, the connection to the rock eased his passage over the chockstone and prepared him for the way ahead.

Above the stone, the chimney dwindled into a boot-sized crack. With both hands pushing sideways against the crack, Todd jammed his feet in, letting them become firmly wedged with each upward step. Fine with two good feet. But how to concentrate with pain needling his left foot whenever he had to move?

One step at a time, he told himself. Let your left foot sink into the rock. Picture the rock flowing around it — soft like jelly. That's what Howie would do.

Todd jammed his arms into the crack above, trying to take some pressure off his feet. The pain was too intense. He couldn't concentrate. He couldn't focus on anything but the pain and the drop below.

I'm sorry, Jess. Sorry, old Howie. I shouldn't have come. Not sure I can make it to the top, and the way down is no piece of cake. Don't trust my belay either — I'm too far above it now.

"You fall because you're afraid to fall." Kurt's words, not his.

"Hey, Todd ..."

Howie. It had to be Howie speaking, pulling him back from the edge. Or was it the wind whispering through cracks, dancing against his eardrums, making fun of him.

"Listen, quit worrying about your belay. You're not going to fall. In fact, you're not going to even think about falling. Take a breather and look at the scenery."

Sure, anything you say, Howie.

It was a relief to stop and let his one foot hang free. Why hadn't he done this before? Now he could see clearly. Straight above his head, where the crack became little more than a groove in the rock, the slope eased off.

"Okay, Howie, I'm ready to go."

No answer. Then go. He didn't need anybody else directing him. Got to get going, got to get going ... Hey, the ridge was flattening out.

Suddenly the rock fell away on all four sides. There was nothing above him. Todd was standing on top of the Witch's Fang. There was nowhere else to go, nowhere to move — he was standing on the tip of the flame. If Kurt suddenly materialized, they would have difficulty finding a place to sit down together. But Kurt did not appear; the north ridge was empty of sound and movement. There was only the whiteness of the Coast Range spread out before him, looking as if it belonged to another Ice Age. How many times had he stood on other summits, silently absorbing the circle of horizon? Usually it had been with Sam or Norma or Jess or Howie. Sure, he'd climbed walls and faces by himself, but never a mountain like the Witch's Fang.

Mechanically Todd opened his pack, laid out a hunk of cheese and several pieces of rye crisp and forced himself to eat. For liquid he had only an orange, which he peeled and ate in sections, making sure no drop was wasted. Afterwards he identified a few familiar peaks, then folded the map and stashed it away. He could imagine his dad's voice rising in excitement, pointing out peak after peak. They had shared this familiar ritual many times. But now he felt no great enthusiasm — only weariness and an intense longing to be back with the others.

He would have to rappel down. Not only was this the quickest and easiest way, but it was probably the one feasible method. The thought of attempting to down climb the crack and chimney with his bad foot made him shudder. First thing to do was find an anchor. Not much choice. There was only the rock knob — the crouching climber he had mistaken for Kurt Stone. Strange irony that his Kurt, frozen forever in stone, should become the anchor.

Todd pulled his climbing rope up. It came without a hitch as he expected. Then he looped a sling around the rock knob and gave a sharp tug. Solid. But to increase the safety margin, he hammered in a piton nearby and suspended his last sling from it. Afterwards he passed the rope through both slings and watched the ends slithering down the crack and over the chockstone. It reached beyond the bottom of the chimney and that's all he needed. Too bad about sacrificing his two slings, but that was the price of retrieving the rope down below.

Before leaving, Todd scribbled his name, Jess's and Howie's names, the date and the route on a scrap of paper and stuffed it into an empty film container. His dad would have added some crummy joke that he had cut from a newspaper or magazine, carefully saved for the occasion. The crummier the better.

Todd placed a few rocks on top of the film container. Not much of a cairn, but there was very little room to manoeuvre. Would his scrap of paper still be there in one year, twenty years? Not that it mattered, except as a passing interest to future climbers. He had not conquered the Witch's Fang by standing on top, nor had he proved anything, except that on occasion a combination of luck, skill, equipment and possibly foolhardiness allows one to walk in the most extreme places. Was he pleased with himself? Maybe. It was difficult to say. Tomorrow, if and when they were all safely down, he might let those thoughts enter in.

Todd took a final look around. Had he forgotten anything? Orange peel and cheese wrapper stashed away, Swiss army knife in his back pocket, extra carabiners clipped into his harness ... His eyes skimmed the north ridge — the visible part — one last time. Strange that there had been no sign of Kurt. He must have turned back earlier on. Well, they would find out when they got back down.

The valley below already lay under the shadow of the Witch's Fang as the dark wave of evening overtook peak after peak on the eastern horizon.

To the west was a solid cloud bank where the sun was fast sinking. Todd shivered. From cold, or a feeling of foreboding? There was something alien about the peak ... something he couldn't explain. Don't be silly, he told himself. You're tired, that's all. And it's time to head down.

Todd straddled the rappel line, passed it across his chest and over one shoulder. There was no need to use a fancier method. The chimney, though steep, was not overhanging and the distance was short. Besides, he had always felt happy using the simple, classic method of rappelling that his father had taught him so long ago.

No reason to stall. He had done it hundreds of times. He could rappel with his eyes closed. Still, there was always that first backward step off the edge and the feeling of abandoning oneself to the unknown. Go then.

With one hand gripping the rope in front of him and the other behind, Todd stepped backward. A few small rocks dislodged by his feet bounded into space. He'd have to be more careful. That meant picking and feeling his way down, legs spread-eagled for better balance. No spectacular leaps or controlled drops — not on the Witch's Fang.

Todd sidestepped the chockstone, pausing only to retrieve the sling and carabiner. His feet danced down the opposing walls of the chimney. What had been a painful struggle going up was taking only seconds. No pain. Only a tremendous sense of relief to be heading down.

I'm gone. You can't get me now. I'm safe. Like a child, Todd felt like shouting his triumph at the Witch's Fang. For an instant he let the rope slide freely through his hands, and he dropped more than a metre.

"More climbers are killed or injured while rappelling than doing anything else, especially at the end of the day." It was his father's voice breaking in, shattering his euphoria.

Todd's hands tightened around the rappel line again, exerting a braking effect. Of course he knew better than to let himself go. Nobody needed to tell him.

His feet touched down on a small shelf some distance below the chimney. Still a metre of rappel line left, but this was a logical stopping place. Todd slipped the rope from his shoulder and pulled one end. Pray nothing got hung up. As the rope snaked down the chimney, a tremendous weight slipped from his shoulders too. He had severed the last link with the top. He was down. Of course he wasn't really down; there was still the gendarme to negotiate, but it was familiar territory. Soon he'd be within shouting distance of the others. Yell, laugh, sing, dance ... He was the all-powerful raven and eagle, spiralling down from the sun-burnished sky.

✧ CHAPTER 11

"COME ON DOWN, TODD." His sister's voice reached out, pulling him back to safety. "We've got some lukewarm chicken-noodle soup waiting for you."

Howie, who was awake and munching on some rye crisp, leaned over and gave him a hug. "I know, you made it. And you're pumped so full of endorphins you can can hardly talk. Like some chubby, happy little cherub descending from the skies — that's how you look."

"Me, chubby? You must be kidding, Howie."

"Any sign of Kurt?" Howie asked after Todd had downed a mug of soup.

"Absolutely nothing. And after being up there by myself for a while, I might have been happy to see anyone, even Kurt."

"Climbing alone is demanding, all right. How was it?"

"There were some dicey sections. It would have been more fun and less nerve-racking with you and

Jess along. I'm beginning to think I'm not cut out for solo climbing, Howie."

"But Kurt was, or at least he thought he was. You know, I'm worried about him. Remember the rockfall we heard earlier this afternoon?"

"You think it had something to do with Kurt?"

"Possibly. I was a bit groggy, but the sound seemed to be coming from the north ridge and certainly the time coincides with Kurt being there."

Todd nodded. "The thought had entered my mind too."

Even if Kurt had been aware of the dangers and realized that the odds against him were mounting, he could never have have resisted the pull to keep going and going, until ... No need to say it aloud, Todd decided, not now.

With the sun finally entombed behind the grey wall of clouds on the horizon, a yellowish pall settled over the ridge and the Witch's Fang. Todd glanced down at Howie's hand. In the excitement of getting back, he had almost forgotten his friend's injury. The new bandage, already bloodstained, looked unhealthy in the yellow light. And Howie, who should have been wrapped up in his own pain, was the very one worrying about Kurt.

"How's your hand, Howie?"

"Could be worse."

Translated, that meant pretty bad. "Can we do anything to help?"

"No prob. Jess put on a nifty new bandage. Afraid I've bloodied it already."

"Yes, and that will cost you plenty," she said, stroking his hand, "because I'll have to put on another one."

Suddenly Todd reached over and hugged his friend. He wanted to comfort him, to tell him that Kurt was already down, that the weather was going to hold, that his hand would feel better in the morning. The silence was stifling. Everything will be all right, Todd kept telling himself.

"Climbing by yourself can be a powerful addiction," Howie said quietly. "I doubt Kurt would have had the willpower to turn back."

"You should know when to quit," Jess countered.

"I'm not arguing for Kurt," Todd said, "but when you're alone, when there's no one to bounce your thoughts off, you lose perspective."

"Nobody has to climb solo."

"Can't you see the attraction, Jess?"

"Frankly, no."

"Take my word for it."

"Pack it up, kids," Howie advised. "Save your energy for tomorrow. I could use some sleep anyhow."

At least seven hours of cold and misery, Todd thought, as he struggled to find a comfortable position for his legs. This was the first time he had ever been caught on a mountain, although he'd been mighty close to it once with Howie.

"Make sure you tie your packs in and keep the headlamps handy," he warned.

Todd caught his breath as he watched the last remnants of light playing over the Witch's Fang. Did she resent this human intrusion? Would she allow them to exit safely? Within minutes darkness would be blanketing them as it had the valley. A long night stretched out before them.

"Wait a second. Before we're all arranged, I need to disappear," Jess announced.

"You would, Jess — these women. Make sure you don't disappear over the edge while you're peeing."

"Save the snide remarks for some other time, Todd."

After she was back in place, Todd checked that everyone was tied in and then spread out the space blankets again. "Better sit on the corners so they won't blow away."

For a while nobody moved or spoke. Todd watched the remaining light gradually filter out of the western sky. Judging by the clouds, the front was still some distance away and any rain or snow would hold off until later tomorrow — at least that's what he hoped. Snow on the ridge would make their descent doubly hazardous.

Although it was completely black to the east, Todd could imagine car lights streaking along the highway, skiers and other holidayers eager to be home after a long day at Whistler or Blackcomb. He shifted his position, moving his pack to better cover the hard rock below. Beside him Howie felt like some knobbly projection of that same rock.

Was he asleep already? Probably. The small stirrings and shufflings coming from Jess's side indicated she was very much awake. Like himself — two minds working overtime.

"Do you believe in telepathy?" Jess asked him suddenly.

"Sometimes I think the notion is flaky, but ask me right now as we're sitting on this ledge and I'd have to say yes."

Jess nodded. "It's weird how people who are far away can seem so close."

"I know what you mean, Jess. I keep feeling Dad's presence, whether I want to or not. And up top it was as if you and Howie were talking to me."

"Exactly. I can see Mom, bent over her radio, listening to the weather report. Don't worry, I tell her. We're doing okay. Just waiting for morning — you down there and the three of us up here. Dumb not to have brought my down socks. My feet are freezing. No, it's not raining or snowing or anything, but the wind is starting to act up ..."

"And while you're at it, Jess, tell her to hold off any rain or snow until we get down."

Todd felt an elbow needling his ribs. "Don't tell me you're still awake, Howie."

"With someone's foot gouging my stomach, a weather forecast going on overhead and you ask if I'm awake? Come on, have one of my hard candies. Maybe it'll put you both to sleep."

They all three laughed, while the darkness and the wind swirled over their ridge. Eventually, in spite of pain and discomfort, they dozed off.

Todd jerked himself awake. Was the air getting warmer? If so, it could signify a weather disturbance moving in. One corner of the plastic blanket had come loose and was rattling in the wind. After tucking it under again, Todd popped one of Howie's candies, plastic wrapper and all, into his mouth. He sat there in the darkness silently praying and flicking out bits of candy wrapper with his tongue. He was talking to the rock, to the drops of moisture on the end of his nose, to Jess and Howie pressed warm against his side, to the Witch's Fang — whoever, whatever she was.

Somewhere between sleeping and waking, Todd dreamed. In his dream Sam was calling through the tent flaps. "Time to stir, Todd. Porridge is ready, and we should be leaving in half an hour."

Then they were running and boulder-hopping across a scree slope. As the slope steepened the rocks began to shift, and they had to use their ice axes for balance. The rocks were flowing round their boots, propelling them down the slope — faster and faster.

"Dad, wait up. I'm too little. The rocks are keeling me over."

Sam held out his hand, but Todd couldn't reach. And the whole slope swirled over him like a stream of lava.

✧ CHAPTER 12

TODD WOKE UP SHIVERING. He felt a headache throbbing where the back of his head had been propped against the rock. On the eastern horizon, the first grey smudge of morning was showing. Not a sunrise to rave about, but at least it wasn't snowing, nor was the wind blowing as hard as during the night.

Howie groaned and stirred. "Where's the stove?"

"In the notch above your head, where we put it last night."

"Can you reach it, Todd? I can't swing my good arm far enough around."

"Sure. How is your hand?"

"Could be better. All night long I've been having the wildest dreams, and in every one I was doing something dumb. I feel guilty for keeping you guys up here, especially now the weather has turned."

"I'm a great one to be saying this, Howie, but you should quit rehashing the accident. It wasn't your fault. The same thing could have happened to any of us."

"I know, but still ..."

"Too bad we don't have any coffee. That would cheer you up and get us all moving."

"As a matter of fact, I did bring some." Howie rummaged through his pack and produced a small metal container full of coffee. "Only a few spoonfuls, but it's real strong stuff, enough to give us a jolt."

"You brought coffee, Howie? I can't believe it." Jess was suddenly awake.

"The problem is water," Todd reminded them. "There's no snow within easy reach, and I have only a quarter bottle of orange drink left."

"My bottle is full from yesterday," Jess said.

"Should be enough for a cup each." Todd inspected the cooking pot. "Oh, great — frozen leftover chicken-noodle soup. How be I warm it over the stove, Howie?"

"I'm not especially hungry."

"Jess?"

"Me neither."

"Over it goes." Todd banged the cooking pot against the rock and watched the noodles taking off. "Something down below will enjoy them."

"It's starting to rain," Jess complained. "I felt a drop on my head."

"You're getting condensation from the space blanket, Jess. No wonder, if you pull the thing over your head."

"It felt like rain," she insisted.

"Any moisture will likely be coming as snow, which is why we have to hurry. Grab yourself some rye crisp and cheese while I make the coffee."

With his one good hand, Howie tried to pour the leftover water into the cooking pot.

"Let me do it, Howie. You're sloshing water everywhere."

"Sorry," he muttered sheepishly. "Nothing is working properly this morning."

"Don't worry. There's enough water left."

Finally the coffee was ready. Todd gulped down the lukewarm brew and watched Jess and Howie struggling with theirs. It would be a chore to get those two moving.

The coffee wasn't helping his empty-stomach feeling either, or the dull ache still hammering the back of his head. In the grey morning light, everything felt unreal, much like the continuation of his own dream. Strange that his foot was bothering him so little after the night on the cramped ledge.

Had this transformation crept over them during the long hours of the night? Whatever the reason, he was the unacknowledged leader now, responsible for getting them moving, for telling them what position to take on the rope, and as leader he would naturally descend last — the only one without an overhead belay.

Todd glanced up at the Witch's Fang. In the lowering cloud and early-morning light, the final spire looked more than ever like a crouching figure

— a climber frozen as he stooped to pick up a rock and place it on the cairn. Todd could feel a numbness creeping over his own body. I can't do it. I'll never get them down safely. They seem half paralyzed by pain, fear, cold ... whatever.

A single flake of snow drifted onto his face and melted. This was something he could understand — snow, wet and dangerous.

We're going down. We're going down now and nothing is going to stop us.

"Let's go, Jess. Take the rope and tie yourself into the lead. I'll go last. That way we can both keep an eye on Howie."

"I haven't finished my rye crisp."

"I'll give you another minute, Jess. Then we have to head down because snow is coming."

Once they started, Todd felt the immediate surge of energy as his heart and lungs took over, pulsing blood to legs and feet and arms and hands. His brain shifted into automatic. It was like directing puppets. If he knew each part perfectly, all would go well: Jess, proceed a few metres down the ridge and stop to take in Howie's rope. Watch that the rope doesn't dislodge any rocks. Howie, get down to Jess somehow, using your good hand. Todd, belay him from above. Now his turn to descend to the others, no belay from above, of course, but Jess and Howie minding his rope. Trust no hold on the Witch's Fang — say it over and over until he was safely down. And now take a good deep breath and start the process all over.

While Todd nursed Howie and Jess down the ridge, mist closed in behind them and a light snow began to fall, blotting out the Witch's Fang.

"Any sign of the flagging we put up where we first came onto the ridge, Jess?"

"Not yet."

"We should be close."

"I hope so."

As he spoke, the mist snaking down the crest of the ridge overtook him, then swallowed up the other two until their voices became little more than ghost whispers sifting through the whiteness.

"I have it," Jess cried out. "I've found our flagging."

"I'll be with you in a minute," Todd said. "Can you see the route below?"

"No. The cliffs and snow gully are completely socked in."

"But you do have the flagging?"

"I tied this red ribbon on yesterday, Todd."

It was reassuring to hear his sister's confident voice again. "Not that I doubt you, Jess, but groping down in this whiteout is disorientating and I need to double check."

Gradually Jess's and Howie's shapes materialized from the mist, a metre or so below him. It was good to latch on to something solid again. The whiteout was making him dizzy, almost sick to his stomach.

Howie held up his mitts. "I've completely shredded them, Jess."

"Never mind. If we ever get off this miserable mountain, I'll make you another pair, I promise."

The three of them straddled the ridge, staring into the void below. Was it better or worse seeing nothing there? Todd wondered. One thing he did know — they would have to rappel directly into the upper gully. With the bad weather and Howie's injured hand, they didn't have a hope in heaven of climbing down their previous day's route.

"Have either of you seen a possible rappel anchor?" he asked.

"I haven't been looking," Jess answered. "Besides, what if our rope isn't long enough?"

He had thought of that too and made some quick calculations after rechecking the map. "We'll be all right with the two ropes tied together."

"Like Jess, I'm not so sure," Howie said.

"I am. I waited in the gully staring up at that sheer rock face for heaven knows how long while you two were climbing. We've got enough rope."

"I'm glad you're so positive," Howie responded.

Was there a trace of sarcasm in his voice? No time to worry about that now. The wet snow was pouring down. At any other time it would have been fun examining the crystal structure as the huge irregular flakes bombed onto his jacket. But not now. Those same snowflakes were coating the gully, turning it into a treacherous highway.

"Look, we're wasting time."

"Sure," Howie agreed. "We'll take your word for it. We're heading down now, aren't we, Jess?"

Jess nodded.

Todd yanked the flagging from the rock and stuffed it into his pocket. If he wanted a belay anchor, he'd better get busy and find one himself or they'd be sitting there forever. The rock where the flagging had been attached — maybe it would do as an anchor. Todd examined the rock, then pulled on it. Nothing moved. He glanced around. Any alternatives were definitely less appealing.

"You'll find my descender in the top outside pocket of the pack," Howie said flatly.

"Let's head on, then. I'll rig up our rappel line and go first. Do you mind coming last, Jess?"

"Doesn't matter. I'll go first, last, wherever you want."

"Howie may need some help," Todd told her. "See if you can fit my leather mitt over his injured hand."

After Todd had tied the climbing ropes together and rigged them to the slings passed around the rock, he let the end slither down and vanish into the whiteness below. The rappel line was ready. Todd gave a few sharp tugs, equal, he hoped, to any force they might exert while rappelling. Not much else he could do. As a last-minute precaution, he took a light line from his pack, attached it to his climbing harness and handed the end to Jess.

"You can give me a belay to begin with."

"And when the line runs out?"

"I'll take it off and you can pull it back up and belay Howie when he goes."

"Be careful," Howie told him.

It was miserable taking the first backward step into space. With the snow falling almost as rain, gaping holes were opening in the mist, like whirlpools about to suck him down. If only there was someone else to guarantee the safety of his anchor, assure him it was bombproof. Todd tensed himself for the first step.

Todd knew he was alone. Yet a voice somewhere was reassuring him. "You've tested the anchor and used a belay line. You've done everything you possibly could, Todd. There's no point worrying."

Todd glanced up, half expecting to see his father's face in the mist. But only Jess and Howie were there, white-faced and waiting their turn.

"You'll come directly after me, Howie? I don't want to wait long in the gully."

"No prob, Todd."

"Thanks for saying it."

Todd checked the descender on his rappel rope one last time. Everything looked shipshape. The rope was running freely around the metal figure-eight, his hand below was ready to brake. In the old days Sam used to recount horror stories of climbers using a screw-type carabiner and wrapping the rappel line the wrong way around, so the rope actually opened the carabiner during the descent. No worry on that account — not with Howie's newest descender.

Todd took a deep breath and stepped off the

ridge. Howie and Jess dissolved into the whiteout, and he became an insignificant speck, gyrating on a yo-yo string. For a moment his feet lost contact with the rock, and like a rank beginner, he panicked, scrambling feverishly for solid ground, before the rope swung him back. He hung there, panting. The rope coiled around the descender was doing its job — the metal felt warm from the friction. He continued on down, feeling his way — blind, except for the rock staring him in the face. Still no sign of the gully, and underfoot the terrain was sheer.

"I wonder how much rope is left?" The sound of his own voice startled Todd. Was his shadowy companion, whoever or whatever it was, listening in?

The light belay line momentarily tightened and held him back. He had reached the end, and one tenuous connection with the others was about to be broken. After untying the line, he let go and watched it slip away.

No voice or sound came to soothe him, except the swish of snow, earthbound. And above him was the Witch's Fang, heavy with snow, and more falling ... Jess and Howie were up there too, no doubt anxious and wondering where he was.

Suddenly he felt ground underfoot. Still steep, but, yes — he was standing. "The gully," Todd called out, knowing very well they couldn't hear him. "I'm in the gully."

He unclipped himself from the rappel line and

flicked the rope, a sign for Jess and Howie that he was down and they should follow. Then he flattened himself against the gully wall and waited. Five minutes slipped by. Still no sign of action. Were they having trouble with the anchor, the rappel rope, Howie's hand? More frightening was the possibility that they couldn't mobilize themselves and were sitting there, waiting for direction.

"Are you coming?" Todd shouted. No chance they would hear him with the distance and the whiteout dampening any sound.

Ten minutes went by. There had to be something seriously wrong. He shook the rope, not a smart thing to do, but it hung lifeless in his hands.

He could do nothing except wait. If only there was some means of communication. His hands were freezing. Probably Jess's and Howie's were too. Snow from the cliffs above slithered into the gully. There would be more where that was coming from, and more and more ... until the Witch's Fang had quenched all their warmth.

Idly, Todd clasped his hand around the rope. A tingling sensation ran through his fingers and the rope started shaking. Someone had to be descending. Whoever it was dumped snow over his head. A few seconds later a figure emerged from the whiteout.

"Am I glad to see you, Howie! What's going on? You've taken half an hour."

"It's Jess. I'm worried. I wanted her to go next, but she kept insisting you told her to come last."

"I did."

"Finally I figured I'd better come or we'd be sitting up there forever."

"You were right."

"No, I should have stayed, convinced her to go next. You didn't see the look on her face."

"I know how she looked earlier this morning."

Todd flicked the rope. "Come on, Jess. Give us a sign of life or something."

Howie grabbed the rope from his hands and shook it violently.

Todd shoved him against the gully wall. "What are you trying to do, Howie? Get us killed? Look at the rocks you've dislodged."

"I should have made her go second."

"You can't *make* Jess do things, Howie. You ought to know that by now, and if you don't you're an idiot."

"You think I'm an idiot for caring about Jess?"

"You've got me wrong."

"I think I understand you very well. You don't care about anyone. All you care about is getting up your damn mountain."

"Howie, don't ... Let's not fight."

"Something's wrong with Jess. I should be up there holding her, keeping her warm. You don't realize how bone chilling it is waiting around."

"I do know, Howie. Will you please listen? Give her time. Maybe she had to find something in her pack, adjust the rope, tie a bootlace, take a pee ... any number of things."

"You're wasting my time, Todd. I'm going up."

"You're crazy. You can't climb vertical rotten rock with an injured hand."

"I'll manage somehow."

"It's too dangerous."

"Let go. Take your hand off my shoulder, Todd."

"Be reasonable, Howie."

"Back off. I'm warning you."

Todd felt a fist smashing into his upper arm, paralyzing the muscle. "Howie!"

"Don't try to stop me. Get it?" Howie reached for the rope, but stopped midway. It was shaking. He spun around to face Todd and said haltingly, "You're right. She must be coming down."

A few minutes later Jess slid into view. "Sorry to keep you waiting. The rope got twisted."

Howie stared at Todd. "I don't know what got into me. Whatever it was, I don't like it. What more can I say?"

"Remind me not to get in your way again."

But Howie didn't smile. "Nothing like that has ever happened to me before, Todd. Can we talk it over later?"

"No prob, Howie."

"What's up with you two?" Jess asked.

"Uh ... I'll tell you later," Howie promised, wiping the snow from her face and giving her a kiss. "Now let's get out of here."

The way down was a nightmare of falling snow and shifting rock. They moved together on the rope, tensed for the slightest sound from above.

Each one stumbled in turn but was held back by the others. And the snow turned into rain, finally skidding them onto the slope below, where they stopped, exhausted.

"Finish the chocolate bar?" Howie asked.

"Thanks."

"Don't mind if I do."

As they stood there, the mist cleared away in patches, leaving them floating high above the valley and the two tents. They gulped down lungful after lungful of the sweet-smelling air.

"Almost as good as water," Howie declared. "And am I ever thirsty."

"Tea with lemon and piles of sugar," Jess sighed.

"And don't forget the soup, Jess — lots and lots of soup."

"Careful on the way down," Todd warned. "I think we better leave the rope on. At the end of a climb it's easy to make mistakes."

With ice axes ready they kick-stepped down the steepest concave section of the slope. Todd held himself and the others in check, until ...

"Yahoo!" Howie couldn't contain himself.

Yahoo ... The echo rushed against the cliffs and woke an answering tremor in the Witch's Fang.

On the lower snow slopes they glissaded — shouting, laughing, occasionally stumbling, and hugging each other when they finally stopped by the avalanche fan. Todd coiled the rope and put it away in his pack. Except for Leo coming to greet them, all was quiet.

Where was Kurt? The inevitable question hung above the snow, crunching closer with Leo's every step. Sleeping in his tent, Todd reasoned, perhaps exhausted and discouraged after an unsuccessful attempt.

"Is Kurt back?" he called from a distance.

"Not yet. I was hoping you guys had seen him."

It was Todd's turn to shake his head. "No sign of him on top or anywhere."

"I was afraid you'd say that. All night I kept hoping he would slip into the tent and I'd wake to find him. No such luck. Am I thankful to see you!"

Todd listened to himself and the others repeating words they didn't believe. "Still a chance he'll come back. What time is it anyhow? Early afternoon. And we're just back. Give him another few hours." Nobody mentioned the rockfall on the north ridge. Time enough for that later.

"Sure, give him a few more hours," Leo repeated. "After a bad night he maybe had a late start. Tired and hungry too ..." His voice trailed off.

"How's your leg?" Howie asked, taking care to hide his own bandaged hand.

"Okay, I suppose. I haven't had time to think about it, what with worrying about Kurt and wondering where you guys were."

Howie patted him on the back. "I can imagine. By the way, when is the helicopter coming?"

"Around three."

"One time I'm actually glad of a helicopter," Todd said.

"And you'll be on it too, Howie," Jess added firmly.

"Who said?"

"I say — we all say." Jess pinned his arms behind his back. "You can forget arguing."

"Whatever you say, Jess. But I need food first. I'm starving."

"As soon as I spotted you coming down, I put on some water. What'll you have? Tea, coffee, hot chocolate?"

"Anything, so long as it's liquid," Howie said.

A few minutes later they were sitting around Leo's stove, sipping hot chocolate from their mugs. The rain had changed to showers and there was a hint of sun behind the clouds. A light breeze was springing up from the northwest.

"Good weather later this afternoon," Todd predicted.

"Good hot chocolate right now," Howie murmured. "This was what I needed. Have you a piece of bread anywhere, Leo?"

"Help yourself from the tent. And there's jam in the tin. Say, I never asked you about the climb. How did everything go?"

"Todd made it to the top. Howie and I waited below because of this." Jess showed him Howie's hand.

"Looks wicked," Leo said. "You should definitely come down in the helicopter with me."

"Feels better this morning," Howie insisted, trying to hide his hand behind the mug.

"You're definitely going down in the helicopter, Howie."

"I second that, Jess."

"Hey, can I eat my bread and jam in peace?"

"Let him eat his bread and jam in peace." Everyone was laughing by this time. "You've got jam smeared on your chin, Howie."

"But seriously," Todd told the others, "we should be thinking about packing up. Did you say three o'clock for the helicopter, Leo?"

Give or take an hour, knowing helicopters. If Kurt hasn't arrived back, I thought I'd leave the tent with his gear inside."

"Good idea," Todd said. "He'll be wet and exhausted."

"Maybe we can get the helicopter pilot to fly over the Witch's Fang," Leo went on. "If we don't see him, I'll contact Search and Rescue first thing. And they'll be back up here later today."

"Do you need help packing?" Jess asked as they were leaving.

"The knee slows me down, but I can manage all right."

"See you later," Howie called back. "And thanks for the food."

Even from a distance their campsite looked forlorn. After shaking some pooled water from the tent roof, Todd retrieved their dishes from a soggy plastic bag. Jess and Howie fussed around, trying to be useful, but accomplishing very little.

"You're too tired," Todd told them finally. "Go on into the tent and find some dry clothes while I fire up the stove."

Todd found the tea bags and settled himself by the stove. Although the Witch's Fang was obscured by cloud, patches of blue kept appearing and disappearing above the ridge. Was Kurt lost somewhere in that kaleidoscope? It was hard to believe they had been there a few hours ago.

Howie was already asleep with his head resting on Jess's arm when Todd crawled inside with the tea.

"I doubt we can wake him," Jess explained. "I barely had time to change his bandage before he was out."

"Well, let him sleep. It'll do him good. Some tea, Jess?"

"Thanks. You know what, Todd?"

"What?"

"This morning I wasn't sure we'd get down."

"None of us were sure, Jess."

"I'm glad we're sitting here, drinking tea. But I can't stop thinking about Kurt up there somewhere. You think there's a chance he'll make it?"

"I suppose there is a possibility he's waiting out the bad weather somewhere."

"I hope so."

"Why not have a quick snooze, Jess? It'll do you good."

A great weariness overtook Todd. He hadn't felt this way since before the accident. It was as if his whole body was relaxing, but instead of sinking deeper into the down sleeping bag, he was rising and floating ... Below him lay the whole Coast Range, horizons disappearing in a blaze of sunlight. And he was the compass. In which direction would he turn? He could feel his body undulating over endless ice fields, sweeping through snow-fed passes, tracking the great glaciers to the sea. Then he was vaulting over the spine of the Coast Range, spiralling and landing face down in alpine flowers overlooking a blue-green lake ...

There's time for everything, Todd realized. He would pack the gear later.

Above his head sunlight and shadow patterned the tent roof, dissolving the showers into an intermittent drip, drip, drip. He could feel himself drifting off. It's raining, it's pouring, the old man is snoring. Rain, rain, go away. His lips formed the words silently — the old verse his parents sang to chase away the storm gods. Good, he'd be seeing his parents shortly.

And while they were resting, the Witch's Fang rose from the mist, and afternoon spilled golden over the peak.

✧ EPILOGUE

THE WITCH'S FANG STANDS UNCHANGED, for a mountain is never conquered by a climber — only the climber is changed. And climbers are not defeated by the mountain, but fail because of their own lack of skill, poor judgment, bad timing ...

Search parties never found Kurt Stone, but several years later two climbers discovered a battered climbing helmet at the base of the north ridge. Inside the helmet were the initials K.S.

A jet trail drifts overhead, a satellite streaks past in the darkness, an occasional ski party tracks below the cliffs ... no matter. Season follows season. Frost, sun, wind, rain and snow work at the rock. Lichen moves a little higher. And somewhere far beyond the fire and ice of human thought, the Witch's Fang will sink below the crust to melt and then perhaps to rise again.